FLOATING ON BAMBOO

Erika Maren Steiger

E. STEIGER & CO.
LOS ANGELES

This edition published 2020 by E. Steiger & Co.
www.esteigerandco.com

Copyright © 2003 Erika Maren Steiger
ISBN: 978-1-951264-01-7

Front cover design by James, GoOnWrite.com

To the patient people of Thailand, who taught me what perspective means, and to the creators and maintainers of foreign exchange programs, who make such experiences possible

Chapter 1

She remembered the first time she had flown into Los Angeles in the dark. Always before, when she had been on a plane alone, it had been in daylight. Maybe that was why she had never noticed how unimaginably big it was.

All the way across the country, the land had been dark, just black, with occasional clusters of lights. When they crossed those last mountains, though, there it was, from horizon to horizon, an unbounded expanse of brightness. She looked in all directions as the plane continued west, but could not find the edge. Finally, where the city met the ocean, there was darkness again. She was surprised to find herself relieved. It was just too much, too many lights, with no boundary. She didn't understand why, since it was just a city, just the place she'd always lived, but it frightened her. She had felt calmer as they descended, and she could see buildings, then cars, then people.

For this trip, the sky was bright, and she was older, but she did feel a breath of fear as they took off. Although she had spent much of her life on planes, she had never gone this direction: west from L.A., over the empty ocean. At first, the water was dark blue. As they went higher, it turned grey, but she could still see the waves. Then they went into the clouds, and all she could see was white.

She turned her head away from the window and toward Ciara, sitting next to her, flipping through the latest Vogue. Tamar could see the March 1985 date on the cover. They had met just three days before, assigned together as roommates for Orientation, at a small hotel near the airport.
Tamar had arrived first, and was sitting on one of the blue and orange beds reading "The Snows of Kilimanjaro" when Ciara bounced in with a big smile and trendy clothes. She was wearing shiny clips in her dark, wavy hair and plenty of mascara and lipstick. She could easily have passed for one of the popular girls at Tamar's school, but when she started talking, just the usual hellos and where are you froms, Tamar could feel that she was different. Her smile was genuine. She was actually interested in the differences between L.A. and Columbus, Ohio, and what it was like to have so many stepsiblings. Ciara's parents were still married. She said they were even still in love.

Ciara was beautiful, although she seemed unaware of it. Her skin was even paler than Tamar's, but somehow, with her very blue eyes and her very dark hair, it looked dramatic rather than pasty. Tamar thought her own brown eyes and red hair gave her skin a jaundiced tinge.

It was odd, the way they had suddenly been friends. It wasn't because Ciara was so friendly, or because they had anything at all in common. There wasn't any rational thought process at all. Tamar just liked her, immediately, from the moment she walked in the room, and the feeling seemed to be mutual, a sort of friendship at first sight. It had seemed like a good omen for the year ahead.

"I can't believe we're actually on our way," Tamar said.

Ciara looked up from her magazine. "I know. Bangkok! Unbelievable. I can't even picture it yet."

"I can't either, and I've seen pictures."

Ciara laughed. "I'll bet you did a ton of research."

"I did! I read everything I could find, which wasn't that much. I still feel like I know nothing about the place at all."

"We'll have lots of time to learn."

"I don't know. Is a year really lots of time?"

Ciara jerked forward as the back of her seat was banged by a knee. It was Joel from New York attempting to get out into the aisle. He was much too tall and bulky for the coach seats.

"Sorry, Ladies," he said as he passed by. "Gotta hit the head."

Tamar liked Joel. Despite his intimidating size and movie-tough accent ("Lawn Guyland Rawks!"), he exuded warmth and a lack of self-consciousness. She envied him that.

Joel was sitting with Ben, a polite boy of average height, with medium-brown hair and Gap clothes. He was a minister's son from a small town in Nebraska, and he hadn't spoken much.

There were eight of them altogether, four girls and four boys. There had been fifty-some at Orientation, but most of them were going to Japan. Tamar was glad she wasn't one of them. Japan didn't seem different enough to her. It was more different than, say, England or France, but it seemed so westernized, and she thought a lot of people there must speak English. Americans were always going there. She didn't know anyone who'd been to Thailand. At school, people didn't even know where it was. They kept asking her when she was going to Taiwan. She was glad to be rid of them and their talk about cars and nail polish. Whatever Thailand might bring, at least it would be different.

The first stop was Honolulu, just a six-hour flight, like between New York and L.A. It was still daylight when they arrived. Tamar looked out the window as they flew low over the water. It was a color blue she'd seen only on travel brochures. It seemed like another good omen.

She thought of when she'd gotten that package in the mail, the one with her host family assignment. She had been so nervous, opening it. It meant the difference between going and not, between escape and another year of inane conversations punctuated with derisive remarks ("Ooh, Tamar got an A. Big surprise. Kiss-ass! Geek!"). Besides, her father was about to get married for the fifth time, and although she was happy for him, she didn't want to be subjected to yet another round of hopeful smiles. She wouldn't mind missing the wedding.

When her parents had learned she was assigned to Thailand, they had both been nervous. The news was full of Cambodian refugees and border skirmishes, and they were afraid for her, but she had pleaded with her mother, daily, using every argument she could think of. She convinced her stepsister Pat to call from college to lobby for her. She even tried to get her little half-brothers to help her beg. Finally her parents had agreed that if she were placed in the city of Bangkok, she could go. She had torn open the envelope thinking Bangkok Bangkok Bangkok, and as she pulled the cover letter free, she scanned it for that word.

When she saw it, she let out a scream, a completely involuntary one. It was like the time she tried that freefall ride, and heard screaming all the way down, only to realize at the bottom that she was the one making the noise. Her mother came running in from her studio, paint dripping from the brush still in her hand, panic on her face. Sam and Noah woke from their naps.

Tamar immediately apologized for making so much noise, but really she didn't care about that, or anything else. She had been placed in Bangkok, which meant she was going to Thailand, which meant she would have the adventure of her life and escape her life, all at the same time. Remembering it now, she felt an echo of that excitement. She stared out the window again so no one could see her smile.

The stop in Honolulu was brief. Next was the long leg, eleven hours to Taipei. It seemed like a treadmill of movies and meals, meals and movies and occasional bouts of sleep. By the time they landed, they were all a bit disoriented. It felt good to get off the plane briefly and just walk around the chairs at the arrival gate. Then there was a short flight to Singapore.

They had to switch planes there, to Singapore Air. An airline employee led them briskly from their arrival gate to their departure gate. On the way they saw the cleanest, brightest airport Tamar had ever seen. Everything shone. They passed a multi-story rock formation, a sort of sculpture with plants and flowing water, and shops for candy, jewelry, clothes, all of which looked expensive. It was like a luxury hotel lobby with Rodeo Drive right through the middle.

The Singapore-Bangkok flight was barely a flight at all. They took off and then they landed. As they taxied down the tarmac, too excited to feel their exhaustion from the 27 hours of travel, Ciara said what they were all thinking: "This is Bangkok. We're in Bangkok. We are actually in Bangkok. This can't be real."

Chapter 2

As she walked through the airplane door into the jetway, Tamar was suddenly hit by the intense, wet heat. There were only a few seconds between the plane and the air-conditioned terminal, but it was enough to feel the weight of the air.

There was a woman from FSA (the Foreign Study Agency, founded in 1920) at the gate to meet them. She was about five feet tall and petite, with straight, black hair in a bun. She wore a light blue blouse and a dark blue skirt. Her shoes were navy pumps. She had black plastic-framed glasses, and her expression was stern. She was fidgety, and kept looking back and forth from the gate to the wider airport, as if they were all about to miss a train.

She kept asking FSA? FSA? as the deplaning passengers filed past, even though she was holding a big sign that said the same thing. With her accent, it sounded like "Eff Et Eh?" Tamar was excited to hear her first Thai accent. She was anxious to learn the language. She wondered what an American accent sounded like in Thai.

When she was satisfied that she had found all eight of them, the woman said, "Welcome to Thailand! I am PiLahng, director of FSA Bangkok. Please come this way. Stay together."

That was their entire introduction. PiLahng took all their passports and had them ushered quickly through customs. They followed her to the baggage claim area, where two FSA volunteers, PiLao and PiJung, helped them get their bags and then put them on a full-sized yellow school bus, just like the ones at home. On the side of the bus it said King Mongkut Teachers' College, in English.

When Tamar stepped outside, the heat hit her right in the face, then spread its wet weight all the way down her body. This was worse than Manhattan in August, exponentially worse. She only had to walk about ten yards, but it was like trying to walk across the bottom of an overheated swimming pool. Every movement took concentration, and the air felt too thick to breathe. By the time she reached the bus, sweat was dripping down her temples and the back of her neck. She found a seat by an open window, and wiped the sweat off her face with her hands. She tried fanning herself, but the exertion just made her sweat more. She watched the others drag themselves up the steps and collapse into seats. No one said a word.

According to Tamar's encyclopedia at home, Thailand had three seasons: the monsoon season, from June to November, the cold season, from December to February, and the hot season, from March to May. They had arrived just at the beginning of the hot season. She thought it had better not get any hotter, because if it did none of them would make it to June.

The bus pulled out of the airport. Its motion created a breeze that lured all the students close to the windows. The breeze lasted as long as the bus was on the nearly empty airport access road, which was, perhaps, three minutes, but then they entered Bangkok traffic, and the breeze was gone.

Tamar had thought that between New York and Los Angeles she was inured to heavy traffic, but now she saw she was wrong. The traffic signals here were nearly useless. There didn't seem to be any lane lines. Even motorcycles had to pick their way slowly around the other vehicles, and for anything larger, there was nothing but gridlock. The one good thing about Bangkok traffic, at least on this ride, was that it gave Tamar an opportunity to take a long, steady look at everything she passed.

There were vehicles she had never seen before. One kind had three wheels and no sides, a seat for the driver in the front and a bench for passengers in the back. It looked like a motorized rickshaw with a roof. PiLahng said it was called a *dtukdtuk*, and was like a taxi, only cheaper. There was something similar, called a *bokbok*, which seated more people. PiLahng said some people used motorcycles as taxis too, but they shouldn't do it because it was dangerous.

Tamar saw a few of them, young women dressed for the office, sitting sidesaddle on the back, holding on to the frame with one hand, holding their bags on their laps with the other. She wondered how they stayed on.

The streets were lined with shops and pedestrians, and there were beggars, too, seemingly everywhere, holding out tin mugs for change. Some of them had missing limbs. For some reason Tamar thought it must be like Calcutta, although she had never been there. She must have seen or read something about it. Maybe it wasn't as bad as Calcutta. She watched people pass by the beggars without looking at them, as if they were bushes or bumps in the road.

Between the people and the vehicles, the noise was overwhelming. It seemed that many of the cars were missing mufflers, and catalytic converters. The fumes were, in some cases, visible. No one wanted to close the windows, though. They were still hoping for some approximation of a breeze.

They finally got it when the bus turned off the main road and onto a nearly empty one. It was bumpy, because it was only intermittently paved, but the heat was less oppressive, and the only fumes were the ones from the bus. After about ten minutes, they pulled into King Mongkut Teachers' College, which did not seem to be in session.

The College consisted of several rundown concrete buildings which reminded Tamar of L.A. high schools. The corridors were all external balconies, the stairs unwalled and outside. A large one-story building in the center seemed to be the dining hall, and in front of it is where the bus stopped.

As it did, the place seemed suddenly to be overrun with blonde and redheaded freckly girls. This was because, of the 71 exchange students, 35 were from Australia, and 32 of those were girls. Some of them had brown hair, and some were more tan than freckled, but it didn't affect the general first impression. There were also ten New Zealanders, three each from Denmark, Norway and Switzerland, and one from the Netherlands. There were four from South Africa and four from Japan. The Americans were the last to arrive, and the others were all curious about them, which is why they all poured out of the buildings when they heard the bus.

PiLahng assigned room numbers and instructed the others to get their new roommates settled in and shown around. Fransje, the very blond, very pale Dutch girl, was one of Tamar's roommates, so she led the way, and helped get the suitcase up the stairs.

There were five beds in the room, one still clearly vacant, so Tamar lugged her suitcase to it and sat down. The other girls trickled in. First was a tall blonde, pretty in that generic WASPish way so misnamed All-American. "G'day," she said, holding out her hand to shake, "I'm Nerissa."

"Nice to meet you. I'm Tamar." They shook hands.

"What part of America are you from?"

"California, mostly, but I've spent a lot of time in New York, some in Florida, some other places."

"Hey, Ro, Tamar here's from California, been to New York."

"Oh, bargain!" Another tall girl, very tan, with short hair, brown but with blonde highlights, and sparkly makeup, walked in the room and then right over to sit down next to Tamar. "I'm Rowena from Sydney. Nerissa's from Melbourne. Noelle over there is from Auckland, New Zealand." She pointed to a short, freckly redhead who had just come in. "Fransje, I'm sure you know, is from Amsterdam. So, Tamar, what part of California are you from? Have you been to L.A.?"

"That's where I'm from."

"Oh, bargain! I have always wanted to go there. My sister's been to New York. She's a model. Some of her friends wanted to go to Disneyland one time, but they never made it. Have you been to Disneyland?"

"Many times."

"I am green with envy. Anybody got a ciggy?"

"I have." Noelle pulled a pack of cigarettes out of her bag. Rowena went over to get one.

"So where are the bathrooms in this place?" Tamar asked the room.

"At the end of the row. I'll show you how to work everything." Nerissa said. She got up and Tamar followed her.

"Oh that's heaps of fun," said Rowena. "You'll love the toilets."

"What's the matter with the toilets?" she asked Nerissa as they walked past several rooms.

"Nothing's the matter with them. They're just different, take some getting used to."

The bathroom was large, like a school locker room. The walls were pale yellow and the floor was white tile. The toilets were in stalls with full doors that went all the way down to the floor. Nerissa opened one of the stalls, and Tamar saw the reason. The toilet was sunk into the floor. It was a regular porcelain toilet bowl, but instead of a pedestal it had a crosshatched projection on each side. "You put your feet there," Nerissa said, "and squat." Tamar scrunched up her nose. "But that's not the worst part. This is how you flush." There wasn't any handle. There was a tank of water next to the sunken toilet, with a plastic bowl floating in it, along with dead mosquitoes and unidentifiable grit. "You take the bowl, and you scoop up water, and toss it in until everything goes down." Tamar scrunched up her face even more, and looked at Nerissa. "It's bloody awful, but I guess we'll get used to it. I'll show you the showers. None of us have tried them yet. We all just got here today."

The showers were a bit more recognizable. Two things were odd. Instead of showerheads, they had faucets, and the faucets were only halfway up the wall, not nearly high enough to be over the head of even the shortest teenager. Tamar was very confused until she saw that there were plastic bowls here too. "What do you do, just run the water and dump it over your head?"

"Exactly, and it's only cold water."

"Oh God! Well, maybe, with this heat, it will be a good thing."

"Let's hope."

They walked back down the corridor. Just as they reached the room, a bell rang. "That's the bell for tea," said Nerissa.

"Tea? Like high tea?"

"Time to eat. What do you call it? Supper?" All the rooms emptied as everyone headed for the dining hall.

It was a cafeteria like any other, with long tables and plastic chairs. The food was served from huge metal containers behind glass, and carried on plastic trays. There were no choices to make. The servers filled a plate and handed it across the glass.

The only utensils were metal forks and spoons, but tablespoons, not teaspoons. The only available beverage was iced tea in a plastic glass. Tamar didn't like iced tea, but she was thirsty.

Dinner was a big pile of white steamed rice, with some kind of meat and vegetable dish on top. When everyone was served, PiLahng stood up at the front of the room and struck a small gong. Everyone stopped talking and turned toward her.

"Welcome to your first dinner in Thailand," she said. "The FSA volunteers and I are going to show you how to eat the Thai way." She held up a spoon and a fork. "This is all you need. You don't need a knife, because everything is already cut in small pieces. It is much easier. Now. You put your food on the spoon to eat it. Very easy." She held the spoon in her right hand, the fork in her left, and mimed pushing food onto the spoon with the fork, and then putting the spoon in her mouth. "See, easy!"

There was some giggling, but no one complained. Volunteers roamed around the room, adjusting the way people held their spoons and forks.

"This is lovely!" Nerissa said. Tamar looked where Nerissa was looking, trying to discern what beautiful thing she was describing, and finally realized she meant the taste of the food. She figured it must be an Australian thing, using "lovely" that way, because Rowena said, "It IS lovely. It looks a mess, but it does taste nice." It was good, salty and spicy, the meat tender and the vegetables crisp. It was a bit greasy, but that didn't detract much from the flavor.

"Very good, everybody." Said PiLahng. "Enjoy your dinner. When you finish eating, bring your dishes to the window, and then go back to your seats. We have more things to do."

"So, Tamar, what can you tell us about Hollywood?" Rowena asked between bites.

"I don't know. What do you want to know?"

"Have you been to the Oscars?"

"No."

"I'd love to go to the Oscars. I'll be a famous actress one day, and then I'll go. Oh God I need a ciggy. Do you reckon I've got time?" Rowena scrambled outside.
Noelle waved to a tall, tanned, dark-haired boy as he passed by with his dirty dishes. "That's Antony," she said after he passed by. "Cute, eh? He's the only Kiwi bloke here. Nine girls and him. I think he likes it."

"What's a Kiwi bloke?" asked Fransje.

"I was just going to ask that," said Tamar.

Noelle's eyes widened. "You've never heard that before? Kiwis are New Zealanders. There's the Kiwi bird and the Kiwi fruit and the Kiwi people."

"And Australians are Aussies." Said Nerissa.

"I'd heard that before, but not Kiwis."

"What do you call yourselves?"

"Americans, I guess."

"That's it? Nothing shorter? What about Yanks?" asked Nerissa.

"No. Some people take offense at 'Yanks'."

"Yeah?"

"It's a regional thing, mostly."

Rowena made it back just as they were all returning to the table. PiLahng struck her gong again. "You may have noticed this is a Teachers' College, and the teachers are having a seminar here for the next few weeks, so, you are all going to your host families tomorrow, and then you will come back here for Language and Orientation Camp. Half of you will come the first half of April, and the rest the second half. I will post a list here of who is in which group. Before you go to your host families, though, we want to give you one important language and culture lesson, so you can make a good impression. For Thai people, it is very important to be polite, so we will teach you just a few things. The first thing, most important, is the *wai*. This is for greeting, for hello, goodbye, thank you, I'm sorry, very important."

She demonstrated the *wai*, hands together as if in prayer, elbows pulled in close to flanks, head tilted slightly forward toward hands. "The higher your hands are, the more respect you show. If you meet the king, your hands should be up high." She raised her hands above her forehead. "If you meet a small child, down here." She pulled her hands down to her chest. "For most people, right here is okay." She raised her hands so her fingertips were just at the height of the tip of her nose. "Now you try."

PiLahng and the volunteers patrolled the room, adjusting hands and elbows. "Good. Good. Now. For hello and goodbye, it is the same thing, very easy, '*Sawatdee*'. Everybody." Everybody said *sawatdee*. "Now. It is different, for girls and for boys. Girls say '*Sawatdee-ka*'." The girls said *sawatdee-ka*. "Boys say '*sawatdee-krap*'." There was general giggling, until PiLahng shot a glare around the room. Then the boys said *sawatdee-krap*. "One more thing. Thank you. *Kopkun*. Girls say *kopkun-ka*; boys say *kopkun-krap*." There were only a few stray giggles this time. "Now. You practice *sawatdee* and *kopkun* with your *wai*. Say hello and thank you to each other." There was more giggling as they turned to each other and practiced.

PiLahng taught them a few more words: *aroy* for delicious; *dee* for good; *kawtoat* for excuse me, *hong nam* for bathroom. Tamar had heard *sawatdee*, and seen people *wai*-ing, although she hadn't realized it mattered how high your hands were. *Pi* was a term of respect, used for just about anyone older, unless they had another title, like *ajahn*, teacher.

PiLahng said there was one more important thing. "Some of you have names that are very strange for Thai people, very difficult. So, everyone will have a Thai name. We picked a name for each one of you, something close to your name if we could. We wrote them on these cards, in English and Thai. You can't read the Thai yet, but your host families can help you."

Tamar's Thai name was Arisa. She was surprised they hadn't picked something with a T and an M in it, but it was a nice enough name. She asked one of the volunteers to pronounce it for her. It sounded like ah-REE-sah-ah. Nerissa's name was Narisa, which seemed a very sensible choice. They walked upstairs practicing their new words, and *wai*-ing each other. Tamar didn't feel tired as she left the dining hall, but by the time she reached her room she was exhausted. Some of the others stayed up talking, but she went right to sleep.

By the morning, Tamar didn't mind the toilets so much. It wasn't that awful, just different. Her big challenge of the morning was to try the shower. She found that wasn't so terrible either. The water was cold, but the air was so hot that after the initial shock, it felt good. She couldn't get all the shampoo out of her hair, but she did end up feeling fairly clean, at least for a few minutes. As soon as she was dry, she started to sweat. It was the best she could do though. She wrapped her towel around her and went back to her room to pick something to wear.

She hadn't had any chance to talk to Ciara, or any of the other Americans. She wondered how they liked their roommates.

She wondered what everyone was doing back home. She wondered what was happening at school. She pushed all of these thoughts out of her head, though, because she had more pressing things to think about. Today she would meet her host family.

Chapter 3

Tamar waited with some of the other students in the shade of a large tree in front of the dining hall. The shade made only a slight difference in the heat, and her nervousness made her sweat even more. She had noticed, riding through Bangkok, that everyone seemed to carry a handkerchief, and she had thought it a quaint, old-fashioned custom. Now that her face was sore from wiping off sweat with her hand, she thought it a very practical thing to do, and was anxious to buy some handkerchiefs.

A black Mercedes sedan pulled up, and PiLahng beckoned to Tamar. Her heartbeat sped up as she stood and grabbed her suitcase.

A man got out of the driver's seat and opened the back doors. From the left side emerged a young woman in her twenties with long hair and flat features. She was taller than Tamar, maybe 5'6". She had broad shoulders and a thick, but not fat, torso. She was wearing a long black skirt and a white blouse.

From the right side came a younger girl, about the same age and height as Tamar. She had very straight, very black hair, cut in a just-below-the-ear bob with perfectly even bangs. The roundness of her face was accentuated by the fact that she was quite chubby. She wore loose-fitting jeans with a long, loose, blue and white striped shirt over them.

PiLahng said, "Tamar, these are your host sisters, Pattanee" she looked toward the older one "and Pattana."

Tamar put down her bags, *wai*-ed as she had practiced, and said, "*Sawatdee-ka.*" The girls returned the greeting, and PiLahng looked pleased. The man, who seemed to be a chauffeur rather than a family member, put Tamar's suitcase in the trunk. Another car drove up, and PiLahng went to greet the occupants.

"You can call me PiJai," said the older girl in thickly accented but quite good English. "This is Chang." She indicated the younger girl, "and this is PiTey." The driver nodded toward her, and she nodded back. "Did they give you a Thai name?" PiJai asked.

"Yes, Arisa."

"How about a nickname?"

"No."

"All Thai people have nicknames. We'll have to think of one for you."

The driver closed the trunk and opened the doors for the girls. Tamar sat in the back with Chang, and PiJai rode in front.

There was air-conditioning in the car. It was such a shock to Tamar that she started to shiver. Her body soon adjusted, though, and she luxuriated in the feeling of not sweating. The ride to the house was quiet. PiJai and PiTey occasionally spoke in

Thai. Tamar watched the traffic. Even that noise was dulled by the closed windows and the air-conditioning.

Eventually, they turned off the main roads, which Tamar now knew were called *tanon,* and onto one of the small ones, called *soi.* It was amazing the way everything suddenly seemed to turn rural. The road was paved, but had no proper shoulders or sidewalks, just dirt and trees, and beyond the trees were rice paddies. About a half a mile down the road, they came to a wrought-iron gate in a high, white wall. The wall had chunks of broken glass all along the top, apparently to deter burglars. The gate opened electronically, and then closed quietly behind the car.

The driveway was perfectly straight, and not very long. To the right was a low wall, about the height of the car, and to the left, a perfectly clipped, bright green lawn, surrounded by flowerbeds and a hedge against the wall. At the end of the driveway was a carport, where they stopped. To their right was a break in the wall that contained concrete steps going up, to their left, a door into the main house.

Tamar followed her host sisters' lead and took off her shoes before going through the door.

They entered into a wide atrium with a marble floor. The house was not air-conditioned, but it had few interior walls, high ceilings, and many windows and doors, and it was significantly cooler than outside. The kitchen was to the right, on the other side of a long counter with stools in front of it. The atrium opened into a sort of great hall with a spiral staircase. From there one could reach a grand living room, with furniture all silk and teak, and the dining room, which was really a dais with an enormous teak table on it. Tamar counted the chairs. There were six on each side, not very close together, one on each end, but room for at least one more, and quite a few more along the walls. She had to stop counting because her new sisters were introducing her to someone.

A woman had come into the kitchen from somewhere in the back. She was about PiJai's height, very sturdy, perhaps fifty years old. Her hair was grey and her skin was leathery. PiJai said, "This is Mehbahn, head servant." Tamar *wai*-ed and said "*Sawatdee-ka*." Mehbahn and PiTey stifled laughter as Mehbahn returned the greeting. Chang fidgeted and PiJai glared at no one in particular. Her face turned red. Tamar guessed she'd made a mistake, but PiJai looked so angry she was afraid to ask. PiJai just said, "Let's go downstairs."

She opened a door, and the three girls walked down carpeted stairs to a furnished basement. PiJai turned on a very loud air-conditioner. The décor here was very different from upstairs. There was shag carpeting, paneled walls, a huge sectional sofa, a glass table. It made Tamar think of The Brady

Bunch. The central feature was a huge TV with an elaborate speaker system. PiJai turned it on.

She changed channels until she came to a Chinese movie, the kind with embroidered costumes and long, white beards, in which everyone does impossible multiple flips and enormous leaps. It was very entertaining, even without English subtitles.

After a few minutes, a young girl came downstairs with some food. PiJai and Chang ignored her, so Tamar did too. She was afraid of making another mistake.

PiJai said the food was mangoes. They were very green, though, and cut in thin slices. They were hard like apples. There was a sauce to dip them in. It was the consistency of vinaigrette, with little red and green circles floating in it. PiJai warned her not to eat any of them. They were slices of chilies, there only to give flavor to the sauce. Tamar followed PiJai's instructions, even though she loved spicy food. The tart mangoes and the spicy sauce made an addictive combination. She had to force herself to stop. She thought dinner might be coming soon.

Another girl about Tamar's age came downstairs. She was very pretty, with thick, shoulder-length hair and a bright smile. At first Tamar thought she was another servant, but then Chang and PiJai said *sawatdee* to her. Tamar said *sawatdee* as well.

PiJai said, "This is our sister Nong." Nong *wai*-ed to Tamar, and she *wai*-ed back. Tamar remembered reading in her

FSA packet that there were two sisters and two brothers, but maybe there had been a mistake.

The others discussed something briefly in Thai, and then PiJai said, "I think we have a nickname for you. Your Thai name is Arisa, and your American name is Tamar (she pronounced it tah-MAHN), so we think Ahn is a good name." Tamar didn't quite understand the deduction, but it sounded fine, so she accepted it. It seemed to make her new sisters happy.

The servant girl came back and said something, and they all got up. PiJai said, "Our mother is home." They all went upstairs, where a woman of about fifty, with thick makeup and sprayed hair and a shiny, heavily embroidered silk dress was discussing something with Mehbahn. She turned toward them as they entered, and the girls all said, *"Sawatdee-ka, Mama"* (accent on the second syllable: ma-MAH). Tamar tried her best to *wai* properly. She wasn't sure how high her hands should be. Mama returned the *wai*, her hands down near her chest, but she didn't smile. She stared right at Tamar, and said, very slowly, and barely comprehensibly, "Wen-come." It took Tamar a moment to understand that she meant "welcome", but then the sisters all smiled and congratulated Mama, so Tamar smiled too and said, "Thank you. Um. *Kopkun-ka.*" Then Mama smiled, and the tension in Tamar's shoulders ebbed.

The dining room table was set, and there were platters of food on the table. Chang said to Tamar, "*gin kao, gin kao,*" while bringing her hand toward her mouth and making chewing motions. Nong took her hand and led her to the table. They all sat down, and then things kept materializing on Tamar's plate, first a big scoop of rice, and then spoonful after spoonful of food. The others kept heaping it on. Every time she looked down, there was something new there. She didn't know what any of it was, beyond meat, vegetables and spices, but it was wonderful. There wasn't one thing she didn't like.

After a while, another woman came in, with two little boys. The woman was about forty, with permed hair and a worried look. The boys were about eight and ten, the younger one with glasses. PiJai said, "Ahn, this is our second mother, Meh, and our brothers Djoh and Djim." This is it, thought Tamar. I'm meeting the second wife. Her FSA information packet had told her the family had three wives. She hadn't quite believed it, but here she was, meeting wife number two. She put down her fork and spoon for the requisite *wai*-ing, and then Meh and the boys joined the table.

When Tamar managed to convince them that she really was absolutely full, all three sisters led her to get settled in. They went out the door by the kitchen, across the driveway, and up the concrete stairs. To their right was a beautiful, Olympic-sized pool, and directly in front of them, a small, two-story building.

The pool looked professional, with lane lines and the depth in meters painted on the sides, and the ground floor of the building looked like two locker rooms with a snack bar between them. There was a metal staircase leading directly to the second floor, though, and that was where they went. They left their shoes at the top of the stairs and went through a door into a sort of living room/study. There was a TV, and large pillows on the floor around it, and a small refrigerator. There were also several desks and a drafting table. There was a door at each end of the room. PiJai said the one to the left was the boys' room. They went to the one on the right.

The room had a high ceiling and tall windows. There were three beds and two vanity tables. PiJai said the bed at the front of the room was hers, and the other two were for two aunts Tamar hadn't met yet. Tamar would sleep with Chang and Nong in the loft. She followed Nong up the white metal ladder and saw three mattresses and a large air-conditioner. The ceiling was too low for standing, but there was plenty of room to sit up on the mattress.

There was also a large spider in a dense web up above the mattresses, in the corner. Tamar tried not to show any reaction. PiLahng had explained that most Thais were Buddhists, and did not believe in killing anything, even bugs. Therefore, spiders were allowed to live and spin where they wished.

Of course, most Thais also ate meat. Maybe the proscription was just about the actual act of killing. Someone had to do it though. Were the butchers Buddhist? Tamar didn't know why these kinds of thoughts always raced through her head. She tried not to think about the spider.

Next they showed her the bathroom. Tamar counted the people who would use it. Three sisters, two brothers, two aunts, eight including her. She resigned herself. She was very happy about several things. There was a lock on the door. There was a western toilet with toilet paper, and the shower had a real showerhead, up high. It didn't, however, have a door, or even a curtain. The entire bathroom was covered in pink tile, and the shower area was sunken a few inches, so one had to step down into it. There was a partial wall, about four feet high, with the sink and mirror on the other side. Maybe the water was contained in the sunken area. The main thing was the flushing toilet. Tamar was thrilled about that.

Her sisters helped her put her clothes in the closet and a couple of cleared-out drawers. As she carried a handful of socks to a drawer, something on the wall caught her eye. It was a *jinjuk*, one of the little lizards that were allowed to roam everywhere, eating bugs. It was cute, like the salamanders in Florida, although she saw those only outside. It held still for a moment, then scurried up the wall. She decided they wouldn't bother her, as long as they stayed on the walls. The spiders might be more difficult.

When the unpacking was done, her sisters took her back to the main house. There were more people there now, and they were all gathered around the kitchen counter, which contained several large bowls of fruit, most of which looked completely unfamiliar to Tamar.

The first thing the girls said was "*Sawatdee-ka, Papa*" (pa-PAH) and Tamar gave her now familiar *wai*. Papa was about the same age as Mama, and about the same height, but thicker. He wore wire-rimmed glasses and a white linen shirt, and he seemed very happy. He kept laughing. He said something that made everyone look expectantly at Tamar. She suddenly realized she was expected to answer him. She tried to register what he had said. It had sounded like, "*Natoo meedoo*." She tried to think of any words she had learned that sounded like that, and then it hit her. English! Nice to meet you! With tremendous relief, she said, "Nice to meet you, too," and everyone laughed approvingly. Luckily for her nerves, that was the end of Papa's English for the evening.

She was also introduced to the two aunts, PiSey, who was in her forties and looked like the female version of Papa, and

PiMee, who looked very old, shrunken and hunched and slow-moving. The third wife was also there. She was about thirty, tall and slim and fragile-looking. She was introduced as PiOhn, and she sat with her hands in her lap, occasionally smiling, but rarely speaking.

Soon, the girls said goodnight and led Tamar back across the driveway. She was glad, because she was exhausted. As they reached the top of the wooden stairs, PiJai said, "Would you like to take a shower?"

"That's okay," she said. "I'm really tired. I'll take one in the morning."

PiJai looked down at the floor, fidgeted a little, and said, "It is the Thai custom, to shower at night and in the morning."

Since it seemed to be important, Tamar said "Okay" and took a shower. It was very pleasant to wash off all the sweat of the day. She hadn't realized how filthy she was. She thought, they must think of me like that stereotype of the greasy European, only I'm the greasy American. They probably thought it was disgusting of her to think of going to bed without a shower, and in that climate, they were probably right.

When she leaned her head back to wash the shampoo from her hair, she nearly fell over. There was an enormous spider, bigger than the one over her mattress, in a web on the ceiling right above the showerhead. It was huge. She didn't know how she could have missed it before. She couldn't leave her hair full of shampoo, though, so she gathered up her courage and leaned back again, thinking, just stay there, just stay right in your nice, comfortable web. I'll be out of here in just a few minutes. She was very grateful that it didn't move. She finished her shower and dried off as fast as she could.

By the time she came out of the bathroom, all ready for bed and in her pajamas, they had turned on the air-conditioning. It was actually cold up in the loft. The spider was still there, right over where her head was supposed to go. Tamar got into bed and pulled the cotton blanket over her head. At least, that way, if the spider dropped down in the middle of the night, the blanket would be between it and her skin. She heard the water start running for PiJai's shower, but within a few minutes, even though the lights were still on, and the air-conditioner was loud, and Chang and Nong were chatting in the room below, Tamar was asleep.

Chapter 4

Tamar was surprised to discover that having one bathroom for eight people caused very little trouble. The only problem was that PiJai would occasionally lock herself in there for more than an hour. Then Chang and Nong would start pounding on the door and yelling, and PiJai would yell back. Eventually she would come out, and within a few minutes everyone would be calm again. Aside from that, it wasn't bad at all. She even began to get used to the giant spider.

Tamar couldn't understand any of the conversations that took place around her, but she was learning a few words. PiJai had taught her how to say "What is this called?" and "How do you say that in Thai?" Mehbahn was more patient with her than anyone else. Tamar would sit at the kitchen counter while Mehbahn worked, and ask the names of all the foods and utensils. Mehbahn seemed to find Tamar's attempts at pronunciation entertaining, and that may have been the source of her patience.

Tamar listened to conversations with intense concentration, trying to discern any patterns. When she went out of the house with her sisters, to see tourist sites like the Grand Palace, or to run errands like picking up some kind of herbal medicine for Mama, she listened to everyone around them. She was able to learn some words that way. She learned *rao* for fast, and *rawn* for hot, and *pang* for expensive.

One word that particularly interested her was *farang*. That's what people called her. When she asked what it meant, she was told "foreigner", but she never heard anyone call the Japanese tourists *farang*. When she tried to press the issue with PiJai, she changed the subject. She wondered if it was a word for Westerners or just for white people. If a white person was born and raised in Thailand, would he still be *farang*? What about black people? Tamar tried to remember if she had seen a single black person since she had arrived. At first she thought she hadn't. Then she remembered a couple of American soldiers she had seen one day. One of them was black. Would he be *farang* too? She had a million questions about that word. She hoped she'd be able to answer them by the end of the year.

One morning, Tamar woke up early, as was her preference, slipped into the shower before anyone else was up, and went down to the kitchen. Mehbahn seemed busier than usual, and there were platters lined up along the counter, some with lettuce leaves or parsley on them. One was piled high with *som*, which were oranges, but small, with very thin, greenish peels. They were sweet, though, and very juicy. They were arranged in a beautiful pyramid, garnished with bright green leaves, so she didn't touch them. Instead she went to the bowl that was always full of fruit, and pulled out a *ngaw*, an egg-shaped red and green fruit with spines like a sea urchin. The thick peel was easy to tear off and the white flesh inside, what little there was of it around the huge pit, was sweet and juicy. It was becoming her favorite fruit. It looked so ridiculous, and tasted so good.

She tried to think of any words she knew that could help her find out what the platters were for. She started with "*Sawatdee*, Mehbahn" and got "*Sawatdee*" in response. She waved her hands over the platters and said "*nee*" (this) "*tuh-mai*" (why). She knew it wasn't grammatically correct, but it did seem to get the meaning across. The answer, though, was beyond her comprehension. Mehbahn tried to phrase it in different ways, but all Tamar could understand was that there was something special about today, a fact she had already deduced from the platters. She smiled, said "*kopkun-ka*", and asked what some more things were called. She purposely said some of the words in the wrong tone, to make Mehbahn laugh. It struck her that if she could do that, she must be able to hear the differences between the tones, and she felt so pleased with herself that she was smiling broadly when PiJai and Chang came in.

She asked PiJai, "What's all this fancy food for?"

"We're going to see our grandmother's grave today."

Tamar's broad smile disappeared. She looked down at her white cotton pants and pink and white striped shirt. "Am I coming? Should I wear anything special?"

"That's fine. It's not a funeral. It's the anniversary of her death. It's a kind of celebration."

About an hour later, the whole family climbed into several cars, heaping platters of food in the trunks and on laps. They drove through Bangkok traffic for a while, and then onto a quieter road. Soon they reached the cemetery, green and hilly, with broad, heavy-topped trees spaced far apart. Near one of the trees they stopped and unloaded. The gravesite was more than just a headstone. There was a wide, concrete platform, about four inches high, with a sloping concrete semicircle, about four inches thick, curled around the back. The effect was of a smooth, grey, concrete stage. Grass-covered ground came up to the level of the back, so it looked as if it had been cut out of a small hill. In the middle of the platform was a large, headstone-shaped slab, with red and green Chinese characters on it. In front of it was what looked like a small stone bench, and on that was an attached stone container full of sand. Mama supervised the arrangement of the platters of food on the platform.

Meh and the boys had gone to the top of the artificial hill, and were decorating it with rolls of crepe paper in a wide variety of colors. Everyone was smiling and laughing. It seemed like a party.

Tamar was baffled, so she just followed directions. Mama kneeled in front of the stone bench, lit three sticks of incense, put them between her hands in a *wai*, and bowed. Then she put the incense sticks in the sand. Papa did the same, and Meh, and PiOhn and PiJai. Then it was Chang's turn, and Tamar was nudged to join her, so she did it too. By the time everyone was done, the stone container was full.

When this ceremony was over, everyone started taking the food off the platform, and eating. The boys lit firecrackers, and laughed when the noise made Tamar jump. It really was a party.

One thing confused Tamar more than the rest, so she asked PiJai why there were Chinese characters on the headstone, instead of Thai letters. She said, "Mama's family is Chinese, from Hong Kong." Tamar wondered if all of this food and celebration was a Chinese custom, or a Thai one, or a Buddhist one. She didn't ask, though. PiJai was running around chasing the boys, and she didn't want to interrupt, and she didn't have the words to ask anyone else, so she just smiled and enjoyed the food.

Most days were much calmer. Papa went on many short business trips, and PiOhn usually went with him. Mama and Meh were always out during the day, and PiJai frequently was too.

Chang and the little boys all had lessons to go to. The swim club was open from 10-4, and PiMee or Nong manned the snack bar most of the time. Tamar was allowed to go swimming anytime, but she preferred to go before it opened, because otherwise the customers stared at her, and some even tried to touch her. She didn't think they meant her any harm. PiMee had a habit of staring at her that way, then taking her arm and stroking the skin on the inside of her wrist, saying, *"peu kao, suay"* (beautiful pale skin). It was complimentary, she supposed, but creepy. She tolerated it from PiMee, but she didn't feel the same obligation to the strangers at the pool. She didn't want to be rude, or even unfriendly, but the attention unsettled her.

She was tired all the time, too. She had known learning such a completely foreign language would be hard, but she hadn't expected it to be so physically tiring. The strain of concentrating so hard on every conversation, trying to pick out a recognizable word or phrase, wore her out, and the heat didn't help. Now she had her own handkerchiefs, and her own flip-flop shoes, but she spent most of her afternoons with a book on one of the aunts' beds, with an electric fan blowing right on her, sometimes reading, but usually sleeping.

One morning, she came into the kitchen and saw PiJai, Chang and Nong sitting on the floor shelling shrimp. It was probably her imagination, but it looked like the shrimp were still moving. She offered to help, and was relieved when they put her to work chopping vegetables.

The preparations were for a party for PiJai, who was graduating from the very prestigious Chulalongkorn University. At least a hundred people milled around the front lawn, talking and eating. The food was wonderful. It was the first time Tamar had eaten *satay*, grilled meat on a stick, dipped in peanut sauce. It was fun as well as delicious. There were curries and soups and crispy fried duck and homemade coconut ice cream. Tamar was very glad she had been sent to Thailand. This food was fantastic. She didn't care how hot it was here. She tried to restrain herself somewhat, because she didn't want to get fat, but she ate at least a little of everything.

There were still quite a few guests there around ten o'clock when PiJai pulled her into a car, along with Chang and Nong and a couple of PiJai's friends. She said they were going dancing at The Palace.

The Palace was like a dance club anywhere, dark with bright, flashing lights and a bass level that made one's bones vibrate. It had a very high ceiling and a mezzanine level that overlooked the dance floor. There were several bars, and tables scattered all around the edges of the room.

The music included American pop, Japanese pop and Thai pop. The Japanese and Thai were similar to the American, only somehow sweeter, more bubble-gum. The dancing was also similar, but it seemed to involve arms almost exclusively. There was not much hip gyration, and almost no bodies pressed against each other. There were just intricate arm and hand movements.

PiJai and her friends did some drinking, but Tamar stuck to soda. After a couple of drinks, one of PiJai's friends pointed to some people a few tables over, and said to Tamar, "You know? That not girls." She looked where he had been pointing. There were several people there, tall and slender and very dressed up, one with a bright blue turban. They did look female. "We call *getuey*. Boy, but look like girl. *Getuey*." Tamar had never seen transvestites up close, at least not as far as she knew. *Getuey*. Well, she had learned a new word.

The next day, PiJai took Chang, Nong and Tamar down to the family's condominium on the beach in Pattaya for a few days. It was calming to get out of Bangkok, away from the traffic and the noise and the pollution, and it was much cooler down by the water. Tamar was still glad to have her handkerchiefs, but she had the energy to do more than lie in front of a fan. From the balcony, they could see the sun set over the Gulf of Thailand, and bright flowers Tamar had never seen before made the air smell like freshly laundered blankets.

One night they went to what was apparently a very famous *getuey* show. The costumes were impressive, and most of the men did indeed look remarkably like beautiful women, but Tamar couldn't quite understand what was supposed to be so exciting about that. It was an entertaining show, but Tamar had more fun on the private beach, listening to the waves.

When they returned to Bangkok, something strange had happened. The servant girls were all gone. It wasn't clear to Tamar whether they were on vacation or on strike, or had just quit. PiJai didn't want to talk about it. All Tamar knew for sure was that suddenly they all had chores to do.

In principle, she was happy about that. She was proud to have been doing her own laundry and making her own lunches since elementary school, and she was expert at dusting, vacuuming and washing dishes. Having servants for everything made her uncomfortable. She felt like a spoiled princess, lounging in front of a fan while the servants swept the floor around her, or eating fruit at the kitchen counter while they set the table.

Once, she had tried to help. She walked in while two of them were putting plates and glasses on the table. She picked up a couple of glasses and joined in. One of the girls stopped moving and looked at her in shock. The other one actually looked offended. Perhaps she thought Tamar was criticizing her work. Whatever the subtleties, Tamar's attempt was clearly unsuccessful, and she never tried again.

Tamar found the announcement that she and Chang and Nong would be doing laundry oddly liberating. Perhaps it freed her from the guilt she felt with the servants around. She didn't realize, however, that they would be doing the laundry by hand.

It didn't look terrible. There were three tubs, the size of inflatable wading pools, one filled with soapy water, and two for rinsing. There was an actual washboard to scrub with. Nong sat by the washing tub. Chang took the first rinse, and Tamar the second. She hadn't realized how heavy wet clothes could be. Within half an hour, her back and arms were aching, and with the number of people in that household, often changing clothes several times a day because of the heat, the laundry took many hours. By the time they were done, Tamar could barely move. When the servants came back the next day, Tamar's gratefulness far outweighed her guilt.

Chapter 5

Tamar was excited to go to the Language and Orientation Camp. She hoped Ciara would be there. She hadn't had much chance to speak with her since they got off the plane. It had been weeks since she had seen any of the other exchange students.

When she first arrived, PiLahng sent her up to her room, just two over from her previous room. When she walked in, someone was already there.

"Noelle!"

"Tamar!" They hugged.

"I can't believe we're roommates again! Do you know who else is in the room?"

"Yeah. Selena and Justine."

"Do I know Selena and Justine?"

"I think so. They're both Aussies. Selena has short, blond hair, plays the guitar."

"Oh yeah."

"Justine's the tall redhead, the vegetarian."

"Oh yeah, with the curly hair."

"That's her."

"So when's tea?"

"Soon, I think."

Justine walked in and said "G'day."

"G'day."

"Hi."

"So where are you placed?" Tamar asked.

"I'm down south," said Justine, "Hua Hin."

"I'm in the northeast, Kanchanaburi," said Noelle.

"I'm in Bangkok."

"Do you like it?" asked Justine.

"Yeah. I mean, I don't like the traffic or the pollution or the heat, but my family is interesting, and everybody's been nice to me so far."

"What do you mean interesting?"

"Well, there are three wives, and an extra sister, and the sister I'm going to go to school with hardly even tries to speak to me, but the other sisters do. Also, one day the servants disappeared and I have no idea why. Interesting."

"Three wives?"

"Yeah. Your families have only one?" Noelle and Justine nodded.

"I read that polygamy is illegal in Thailand," said Justine.

"Well, no one told Papa."

The bell rang, and they rushed down to dinner. Tamar looked around for Ciara, but didn't see her. Noelle spotted Selena, so they sat down next to her. She was sitting with Ben from Nebraska, and Duncan, one of the three male Aussies.

Duncan was of slight build, very tan, with curly blond hair. He played folk music on his guitar and liked to talk about Buddhism and surfing. He was already the object of several crushes. He and Ben were rooming together.

"A fellow American!" Tamar said as she sat next to Ben. "We're drowning in a sea of Aussies, and the occasional Kiwi."

"G'day mate!" Ben said, in an exaggerated Aussie accent.

"Time for tucker!" Tamar replied, in kind.

"Fair dinkum?"

"Fair dinkum, mate."

"Well, gee, partner, I reckon it's time for supper." Said Noelle, in an equally awful American accent.

"Who was that? John Wayne?" asked Tamar, laughing. "Besides, you guys say 'reckon' not us."

"You don't say 'reckon'?"

"Not since, I don't know, 1894 or something."

"Hunh." Noelle took a bite of her dinner. "This curry is lovely."

"It really is." said Tamar. "I hate green beans but I'll eat these."

"There's Rowena." Noelle waved toward a table across the room. Rowena was indeed there, and sitting with her were three other Aussie girls and Ciara all waving at them. Tamar waved back enthusiastically. She planned to go talk to Ciara when dinner was over, but in the confusion of clean-up she lost sight of her.

That night, Selena and Duncan sat on the steps in front of the dining hall and played their guitars. They played James Taylor, Simon and Garfunkel, the Eagles. It was just like summer camp. Selena also played some of her own songs. They were folky, with little drama, very gentle songs. Her voice was gentle too, soft but clear.

At one point, the musicians and their audience were distracted by raucous laughter and swearing. Rowena, Ciara and the girls they had been with at dinner were stumbling toward one of the dormitory buildings. They had at least one bottle with them.

Somebody said, "PiLahng's going to catch them if they don't shut up."

"Where did they get liquor anyway?"

"I thought it was Nerissa who brought it."

"No, it was Rowena."

"Well, whoever brought it, they've all been drinking it."

"Let's forget about them and sing something."

The next morning, nobody talked about the night before, because the lessons started. They were divided into small groups and rotated through Thai Language, Thai Culture, and English and Cultural Activities. Tamar and Ciara were not in any of the same groups, so they didn't see much of each other. Instead, Tamar spent much of her time with Ben and Duncan and Selena and Noelle.

In Thai Language, they learned the alphabet, 44 consonants and many, many vowels, and the grammar rules, which were mercifully few. There were no declensions or conjugations, and there was very little use for articles or prepositions.

Tamar said to Noelle, "Once you get past the tones, Thai is really pretty easy." Noelle stared at her for a minute. "So, when do you get past the tones?" They had to practice them over and over. "Mee, mee, mee, mee, mee. Mah mah mah mah mah." It sounded like vocal exercises. The names of the tones, high tone, low tone, rising tone, falling tone, just made it more confusing, because the high tone falls, and the falling tone rises, so the names were hard to keep straight. The other tricky thing was the word order. The teachers all used the same example: *dee jai* (good in the heart) means very happy, but *jai dee* (heart that is good) means kind.

In Thai Culture, they learned more subtleties of *wai*-ing, and the importance of keeping your head lower than the heads of all your social superiors. The intricacies of hierarchy were very confusing, but since Tamar was both young and female, she could count on being inferior to just about everyone, which meant a lot of slouching. They also learned about the low status of feet, and the importance of not pointing your soles at anyone, or stepping over people. It was also an extreme show of disrespect to touch someone on the head, especially an image of Buddha.

They also learned the basics of the dramatic curves and bright colors of Thai art and architecture. It was ornate, but somehow never overdone or tacky. They heard and saw the rhythms of Thai music and dance, and they learned that *Thai* means free, and that the very long Thai name for Bangkok, which is generally shortened to *Krung Tep*, means something like City of Angels.

Tamar found this to be a remarkable coincidence, since she came from the land of the free and the city of angels. She wondered why people who live so differently would choose the same names. She thought about what being from the land of the free meant. Did it mean the same things here as at home, or was it different? One thing she did know it meant was that Thailand was the only Southeast Asian country never to have been colonized by Europeans. When the *ajahn* said that, she stood up very straight, and her voice was very clear.

The English and Culture classes were much less pleasant. They were brought in their groups to classrooms at a local school, without preparation, and told, essentially, to perform for

48

the students. They were supposed to teach them songs and games in English, but it was very difficult, because the students' command of English was limited to "Hello" and "Thank you". It was particularly difficult for the Japanese students, because even though they had studied it in school for many years, their command of English was equally limited. The Europeans spoke perfect English, but they didn't know many songs, other than pop songs. The result was confusion, discomfort, and frequent renditions of Waltzing Matilda and America the Beautiful.

The Language and Orientation Camp didn't increase Tamar's working vocabulary much, but it did help her better understand what she had learned. For instance, she now knew that the phrase, touted as a sort of national saying of Thailand, which she had heard as *"mai pellai"*, was *"mai bpen arai"*, literally "no is what" or "it's nothing", most frequently translated as "no problem." When people actually said it, however, which they frequently did, it sounded like *"mai pellai."*

Tamar thought she must sound like the cab drivers and 7-11 attendants in America who said "gonna" and "hafta", with heavy accents, their attempts to sound like the natives just making them harder to understand. She resolved to speak a bit more distinctly.

Near the end of the camp, though, was the Thai holiday of *Songkran*, the Water Festival. PiLahng warned them that they would get very wet. Since the heat had only intensified through April, they were all looking forward to it.

When they arrived at the school that day, about twenty of the young girls were dressed in traditional Thai costumes, the baggy, folded-over pants, and the crepe sari-style top, in full makeup, with their hair slicked down, performing a dance. At the end of the dance, there was some kind of ceremony, in which the girls poured water over the hands of several adults, presumably teachers.

From that dignified beginning, the entire schoolyard rapidly reached a chaotic frenzy. There were crowds at all faucets, as students filled buckets, balloons, waterguns, hats, any available container, with water, and then splashed any reachable target. It was just a huge waterfight. There was laughing, screaming, a few minor injuries. Even PiLahng and the schoolteachers joined in a little bit.

By the time they all got back on the bus, their hair and clothes were dripping, and they were exhausted, but almost cool. They even caught a breeze on the way home that gave some of them a chill. PiLahng ordered them to get out of their wet clothes before dinner, but most of them procrastinated.

Tamar sat with Noelle and Nerissa and about ten other students under a big tree, enjoying not sweating for a while in their cold, wet clothes. Gradually the group shrank, as one or two at a time went inside. Eventually the group was reduced to just Tamar and Ben, from Nebraska.

They could see a big group of people sitting in the driveway, laughing. Ciara and Rowena were at the center of it. "I wish I could be like that," Tamar said.

"Like what?"

"The center of things, keeping everyone's attention, making everyone laugh, having everyone like you."

"You don't have to be a showoff for people to like you. Some people don't like that at all."

"I don't think they're showing off. I think it's just the way they are."

"Well, if it is, I don't know why you'd want to be like them. Come on, it's almost dinnertime. We'd better get changed."

Chapter 6

Soon after her return from camp, Tamar's sisters took her shopping. She had been to Central Plaza (sen-TRAN pla-SAH), the big, air-conditioned department store, but today they were going to the real market. PiTey dropped them near an enormous pile of *som*. The market was just booth after booth after booth, like a street fair. There did seem to be some logic to the arrangement, fruit sellers together, clothing sellers together, etc. Next to the lady with the *som* was another with *ngaw*, and another with thick purple *mongkut*, and more with all the other bewildering fruits of Thailand. Next they passed souvenir knickknacks, little wooden elephants, and fake ivory carvings. PiJai became very interested in the clothing booths, began negotiations a few times, and finally bought a shirt. Tamar watched her technique. It was aggressive, and even seemed rude. She put *ja* at the end of every sentence. *Ja* was sort of the opposite of *ka*. It could be a term of endearment or something one said to little kids, but like this, between adult strangers, it meant "I am superior to you." PiJai used it with the servants at home, too.

Tamar was not excited about having to talk to people like that, but if that was the culture, perhaps she'd have to learn.

She was relieved when Nong bought a bead bracelet using a very different technique. She smiled, spoke softly, and still got the price down from fifty baht to fifteen. Chang finally bought something too, a cassette tape of some Japanese pop star. Her technique was sort of a watered-down version of PiJai's. She used a lot of *ja* too. They all kept asking Tamar if she wanted anything, but she really didn't, and she wasn't quite ready to try bargaining yet. She preferred just having set prices, less hassle.

Whenever she was out, she heard that word, *farang*. She still wasn't sure if it was neutral or not, but it certainly wasn't complimentary. It seemed that it could be neutral sometimes, just a statement of fact, but in certain contexts, it seemed to lean toward the derogatory. She still wasn't sure.

There was a horrible smell as they approached the meat section of the market, but even the intensity of that stench did not prepare Tamar for the sights. There were skinned pig's heads hanging from hooks, other creatures hanging whole, or lined up on counters, some dripping blood. There were fish in plastic-lined boxes, flopping around in their death throes, shellfish crawling over each other in buckets. There was flesh and death everywhere, and flies crawling on all of it, and the corridors between the booths were so narrow that Tamar could barely avoid touching the animals, and the smell, in that heat, was excruciating. Tamar was afraid she would throw up, but it didn't seem to affect the other girls at all. She supposed they were used to it. This made it even harder for her to understand why they wouldn't kill spiders.

It took them several hours to work their way through the market. The first McDonald's in Bangkok had just opened, and PiJai took them there for lunch. Tamar would have preferred something a bit more authentically Thai, but she was curious to see if it was any different from McDonald's at home.

It was more or less familiar, but it was huge, with high ceilings, and very clean. There were employees everywhere, some just standing around waiting for someone to drop or spill something. There did seem to be something a little different about the way the hamburgers tasted, but Tamar wasn't sure. It might have been her imagination. They had pineapple pies instead of apple pies, but other than that, the menu was the same. The place was very crowded, and with Thais, not foreign tourists.

Outside were more beggars. At first Tamar had disapproved of the way her sisters walked by them as if they didn't exist. Occasionally she had dropped a baht in a cup. She was beginning to see, though, how ubiquitous the beggars were, and how that made ignoring them the only reaction possible. There were just so many, sometimes huge crowds in one place, and sometimes aggressive crowds. You couldn't give every single one of them a baht, and even if you did, what good would that really do? They'd still have to beg tomorrow. She tried to think of what would actually help them.

The plight of the beggars soon faded to the back of her mind, though, because after lunch they went to a movie, a Thai movie. There were American movies in town, too. Tamar had seen posters for Rambo, and one of those stupid teen bikini movies. This one was about a pair of tragic lovers. Tamar could understand only bits of the dialogue, but the story wasn't hard to follow. The man had to go away to Japan for some reason, and they wrote letters for a long time, and then there was some problem between their families, and other melodrama. They didn't end up together in the end. It was somewhat entertaining. Tamar focused on trying to pick up words. The word "*jai*", heart, was used a lot.

After the movie, Nong and Chang begged PiJai to let them "*bpai dun-kin*." Tamar knew *bpai* meant go, but she had never heard *dun-kin* before. Since they were so excited about it, she thought it might be some kind of game, or a special store. It turned out to be Dunkin' Donuts, a great big orange and pink store, just like at home. It was full of teenagers, some of whom Nong and Chang greeted. Apparently it was the cool hangout spot. They each ate a donut, and then PiJai insisted they go meet PiTey and go home. Tamar was glad. She felt as if she had been walking around Bangkok for three or four days.

The next day, Mama asked a question at dinner that Tamar didn't understand. PiJai explained that Mama was going to the temple the next day, and had invited Tamar to go with her. She readily accepted. She wanted very much to know what a service at a Buddhist temple was like. She nodded and said, "*kopkun mahk-ka.*" Mama then said something to Chang that made her look mopily at her plate. Tamar was afraid she had made another mistake, but Mama looked pleased, and she wanted to go, so she decided not to worry about it.

Following PiJai's instructions, she wore white. She was glad her white pants had just been washed, again very grateful she hadn't had to scrub them herself.

Chang came too, also in white, but she didn't seem in a very good mood. She spoke even less than usual, and kept looking down. Mama was full of energy, though, and smiling.

PiTey drove them to the temple grounds, which looked like a big park. The grass was all trimmed, and there were paths lined with flowerbeds leading in many directions. There were perhaps 300 people milling around, and more arriving.

Their first stop was a long table overflowing with platters of food, to which they added a few. It seemed to be for donation purposes, maybe for the monks to eat.

They followed one of the paths to what seemed to be the focus of the crowd, a long one room building, or rather a pavilion. It had no walls, only pillars and a roof. At one end was a platform with a chair on it, and all draped in what looked like silks. An elderly monk in a toga-like orange robe sat on the chair. It looked like a throne.

There were other monks around him, and he was chanting into a speaker system. Tamar couldn't figure out if he was speaking Thai or some ecumenical language. Whichever it was, she couldn't understand any of it. There were rows of people sitting on the floor of the pavilion, facing the elderly monk. They must have arrived very early. The other people were all sitting on the grass, facing the pavilion.

Mama had been foresighted enough to bring blankets for them to sit on. She demonstrated for Tamar the proper position. It was like sitting sidesaddle on the ground, legs to one side, torso forward, hands up in a *wai* position. It was not at all comfortable, but Tamar could see from the behavior of the other participants that it was acceptable to switch sides from time to time, and, having been to various kinds of religious services before, she assumed it would only be for an hour or two.

It was much more than an hour. In fact, it lasted all day. There was a lunchbreak, for which Mama had brought food in Tupperware containers. Several people came by to say hello. Mama introduced Tamar to them, and looked very pleased when she *wai*-ed properly.

There didn't seem to be any ceremony, like communion or baptism or carrying the Torah around. It was just sitting and chanting, all day. Tamar began to understand why Chang had been reluctant. She was glad she came, though. Now she had been to a service at a Buddhist temple. She had some difficulty standing up and straightening her legs when it was time to go home, but she still counted it a good day.

A few days later, Tamar was spending the afternoon reading in front of a fan, when suddenly a breeze seemed to come in through the window next to her. She turned off the fan and leaned out the window. The sky was darkening, and leaves and small twigs were floating by in the air. The breeze gradually became a small wind, and then, as if someone had unzipped the clouds, water fell, fast and heavy, drenching everything. She saw one of the servant girls run into the kitchen, so wet her clothes seemed to be falling off. It poured for an hour or so, never reducing in intensity, sending beautiful cool air in through the window, and then it stopped. It didn't slow down at all. It went full force for an hour and then stopped, as if it worked on an automatic timer. The heat came back very quickly, and the sun had dried everything by dinnertime, but it had been a wonderful hour. Monsoon season wasn't supposed to start until June, and it was barely May, but there was no doubt the rains had come.

After that, the rain came predictably, every day, at about 3 p.m. At first Tamar was stunned every day by the reliable punctuality of it, but after a week or so she came to expect it, like everyone else. She noticed no one carried a raincoat, and few carried umbrellas. People did duck under cover when the rain came, but some just kept walking and got wet. It was a great relief from the heat, like a daily *Songkran*, and the sun dried you quickly afterward. The heat didn't seem any less than it was in April, except for that daily break. The best part was right before the rain, when the sun was dimmed and the breeze started up, gradually increasing. Tamar decided she loved monsoon season.

One morning, PiJai answered the phone, spoke for a few minutes, and then said to Tamar, "That was PiLahng. She wants you to come to the FSA office. PiTey is with Mama, shopping, but they should be back soon."

"That's okay. I can take the bus." She was excited about having the chance to go somewhere on her own.

"I don't think it's a good idea. PiTey will be back soon."

"I can do it. I've got a map with all the routes, and the #93 goes straight from here to a block from the FSA office. I've got money for the fare. I know how to do it. They showed us at Language and Orientation Camp. Really, I'll be fine. I used to take the bus by myself at home all the time. I promise I'll be fine."

PiJai continued to protest, and Tamar to reassure, as she combed her hair, grabbed a handkerchief, some money and her map, put on her flip-flop shoes, and headed down the stairs and the driveway and through the little pedestrian gate in the wrought-iron fence.

There she was, on the dusty road, heading for the bus stop, by herself. This taste of independence was exhilarating for her, and yet she felt calmer and more relaxed than she had in weeks, perhaps months. She felt ready to be out on her own, at least a little. She could understand most of what people said to her now. She was still restricted to a very few phrases in her speech, but she could understand quite a lot. It was generally very frustrating, but sometimes fun, because people would say things in front of her she wasn't supposed to hear. She wondered if people on the bus would talk about her.

There were a few people at the bus stop when she got there, an old woman with a bag of *som*, and a couple of university students. When the #93 came, she saw none of them were flagging it down. She stepped out into the street, put her arm out straight at a 45-degree angle to her body, and made that motion, like patting a dog on the head, that was the Thai equivalent of waving for a taxi. The bus slowed down, but she knew it wouldn't completely stop, so as soon as she could, she jumped on, feeling a great sense of accomplishment at having gotten that far. The bus was, amazingly enough, not very crowded. There weren't any free seats, but the aisles weren't crowded at all. She grabbed a pole near the back door, in the middle of the bus.

The conductor made his way down the aisle, clicking his cylindrical metal ticket and change machine. When he got to her he said, "*song baht, song baht*." She gave him two baht, and he gave her a little square ticket, of that same flimsy paper that bus transfers were made of back home. Now she had made her first transaction completely in Thai, and all by herself. She couldn't wait to go to the market for bargaining.

She knew they would go a long way down *Tanon Chulalongkorn*, and it wasn't until they turned off it that she'd be nearing her stop, so she relaxed and looked at the traffic and the people on the streets. It made her very happy that it all looked very familiar.

Once the bus turned, she got nervous. She was afraid to miss her stop, but she saw it, rang the bell, and hopped out the door as the bus slowed down. As she walked toward the FSA office, she felt like an expert on Bangkok, practically a native.

Chapter 7

When Tamar arrived at the FSA office, Ciara, Ben and Joel were already there. She and Ciara hugged and said how great it was to see each other.

"Do you know what this is about?" Tamar asked.

Joel said, "PiLahng said something about a dance."

"A dance?"

PiLahng came in the room. "Yes. There is a Thai-American dinner next month. You are the U.S. students placed in Bangkok, and you are going to dance."

They all looked at each other in terror.

"What kind of a dance?" Tamar asked.

"Thai dance. Folk dance. Very easy. Come upstairs. The teacher is here to show you. Very easy! Don't worry!"

They all inched up the narrow stairway behind PiLahng. In the library was a tiny woman with a graceful neck and delicate fingers. When she moved toward them, it was less a walk than an ocean swell. She arrived smoothly in front of them, the hem of her skirt settling around her ankles like seafoam blending into sand. PiLahng said, "This is PiEng." They all *wai*-ed and *sawatdee*-ed. She looked them over. Her face was kind, her eyes soft, but, just being in the same room with her, they all looked relatively bulky and awkward, and they knew she knew it. Tamar was the smallest of the four, but she was several inches taller, many inches thicker, and defeatingly less graceful than PiEng.

PiEng spoke no English, but luckily, by this time, they could understand "this way", "the other way", "look up", etc. The dance was fairly simple, a folk dance from the northeast about fishing. They just had to run and hop and move small nets back and forth and up and down. PiEng made them do it until they knew the basic steps. Then PiLahng said they should practice at home and come back the same time the next week.

As they went down the stairs, Tamar said, "I felt like a hippo."

Ciara said, "*You* did? I was afraid I was going to step on her."

"It wasn't that bad. It was sort of fun." Said Ben.

"I felt like an idiot" said Joel.

"It was kind of fun," said Tamar, "but do you have any idea how many people we're going to have to perform in front of?"

No one did. Joel said, "Let's forget about it and go get something to eat. Have you been to any of these *gutio* places?"

Ben and Ciara nodded.

Tamar said, "No. My host sisters only want to take me to McDonald's and Dunkin' Donuts."

Joel laughed. "Don't you ever get out by yourself?"

"This is my first time. They're really protective. I had to fight to take the bus today, instead of waiting for the chauffeur."

"Food first, and then I want to hear about the chauffeur."

They walked down the *soi*, and soon turned onto a *tanon*.

"So your house isn't full of servants?" Tamar asked Joel.

"We've got a maid."

"We've got a chauffeur, a head-servant, Mehbahn, and four or five servant girls. It changes. There's kind of a high turnover."

Ciara said, "I don't even know how many there are at my house. I think it changes pretty often, but there are four houses, so maybe they're just at different ones on different days or something."

"Whadya mean, four houses?" asked Joel.

"For the four wives, I think."

"We have two houses, but all three wives live in the same one," said Tamar.

"I'm moving in with one of you," Joel said.

"What about you, Ben?" Ciara asked.

"My family doesn't have any servants."

"Here it is," said Joel, "*gutio*!"

They walked into a stall with a few tables and a big steamy counter in the center, a cross between a bar and a popcorn machine, with noodles of various textures and thicknesses behind glass. They each bought a five-baht bowl of soup with their choice of noodles in it. This was the one dish Thais ate with chopsticks. The chopsticks were for the noodles. For the soup, there was a deep, flat-bottomed spoon. They sat at one of the tables and tried not to splatter each other. Ben was quiet, but Joel was as energetic and talkative as usual. The other customers stared at them, four *farang* at a *gutio* stand, one of them big and loud.

"Pretty good for five baht" said Tamar.

"This stuff is great," said Joel. "I eat it all the time."

"So have you been all over Bangkok already?" Ciara asked him.

"Not all over, but I go out a lot. My family just has little kids. They want me to teach them English, but other than that, they pretty much leave me alone. They're great."

"I think a lot of families want us here to teach their kids English," said Ciara. "My host sister always wants to speak English with me."

"Mine stick mostly to Thai." said Tamar. "One sister speaks good English already, which helps me a lot sometimes, but the others don't at all, really, although Papa and Mama both try. Luckily I don't see them much, especially Papa."

"Why don't you see him?" asked Ben.

"He's always on business trips. He and PiOhn, the third wife, travel all the time."

"Oh. My family just stays home. There's only one wife, and they all always speak Thai. I help the kids with their English homework, though."

"How many kids are there?" asked Ciara.

"Six. Two girls and four boys."

"Wow. I just have one host sister. I think there's an older brother, but I haven't met him."

"I'm not sure what the deal is with my family. Mama has two daughters, and Meh, the second wife, has two sons, but there's this other sister, Nong, and I don't know who her mother is. Maybe she's not really a sister, maybe a cousin or something. I haven't figured it out."

"Weird."

"Yeah."

"Well, my family's not confusing at all," said Joel. "There's one husband, one wife, and two sons. It's very simple."

"That sounds much easier," said Tamar.

"Easier, but less interesting. I want to hear more about all these wives. That four women in four houses deal sounds pretty good."

By the time they finished their *gutio*, it was after four and Tamar thought she had better head home. She and Ciara exchanged phone numbers and promised to call each other, then she said goodbye to all of them and walked to the bus stop. She caught the bus easily, and even though it was much more crowded this time, she managed it expertly, and arrived home well before dinnertime.

Chapter 8

School began in mid-May. Tamar would be in Chang's class. Nong went to a different school. Her uniform made Tamar feel seven years old. It consisted of a white button-down blouse with a peter pan collar and puffy sleeves, a navy blue pleated skirt that fell to mid-calf, white ankle socks and black maryjane shoes made of some kind of plastic or rubber. The girls' hair had to be either shorter than chin length or up in pigtails. Makeup was not allowed, and shaved legs were considered freakish. Tamar was happy to keep her hair short, and the rest wasn't that bad either. She had wanted something different, after all.

Tamar spent extra time trying to learn her Thai letters. There were some children's books around the house that helped her read a little, although she found Thai much harder to read than to speak. It was hard for her to remember which letters indicated which tones. She came across something that startled her, though. Her sister's name, Chang, seemed to be the same as the word for elephant, *chang*. Chang was a little chubby, but would her family really call her something like that, all the time? Maybe it had some other connotation, like good memory, or strong. The way PiJai said it sometimes, though, it didn't seem that way. Tamar spent a few days trying to figure out some way to ask about it without offending anyone, but then Chang said something to her that seemed to answer the question. She said, with her head down and her fingers fidgeting, "*Tee rongrien, chun cheu Pat.*" At school, my name is Pat.

That was all she said, and then she walked away. Tamar thought it was cruel of her family to call her Elephant, but maybe it didn't seem so bad in Thai. At least she wouldn't be called that at school. Tamar decided to call her Pat all the time.

On the first day of school, PiTey dropped Tamar and Pat at the entrance to a *soi*. There were two lines of uniformed students, one of boys and one of girls. The boys' uniforms were similar to the girls', but with bermuda-length shorts instead of skirts.

The lines were for some sort of vehicle. It was like a delivery truck, a UPS truck, perhaps, but it had no back doors. The back was completely open. The cargo area was empty but for two benches, one along each side. A truck would stop, and students would file in, girls on one side, boys on the other. When it was full, the truck would head down the *soi*, and another would pull up to the end of the line.

Following Pat's lead, Tamar stood quietly in line until their turn came, then climbed up onto the girls' bench, and sat, still quietly, knees together, hands in lap, as the truck rattled down the *soi*.

There were no windows, but out the back of the truck she could see the buildings along the main road, then a bridge, then, immediately, fields, just green, for what seemed like miles. Occasionally she would catch a glimpse of a small wooden building, or some people working. They wound around through the fields for half an hour at least, and then the truck stopped, and everyone filed out.

The school was three stories high, similar in design to the Teachers' College, with the corridors on the outside. In front of it was a large paved area, with a tall flagpole and three flags. Tamar recognized the Thai national flag, but not the other two.

The students were all in lines in the paved area. Pat led Tamar over to the line for their class, and started a discussion with the other girls. They spoke quickly, without much enunciation, and Tamar could only understand a few words. She looked around at all the well-behaved, quiet students standing in their lines, and wondered what happened next.

A bell rang, a very loud bell, and there was an announcement over a poor quality PA system. The students all put their hands together in a *wai*, so Tamar did too. They said some sort of a prayer, or a pledge, and then something else, and then sang a song, probably the national anthem. Pat said it was the same every day. They called it *kaotao*.

At the end of *kaotao* there were more announcements, and then the classes started filing to their classrooms. Tamar knew from Language and Orientation Camp that, except for art classes and dance classes, the students stayed in one classroom, and the teachers moved from class to class.

Their classroom was on the third floor. They all left their shoes lined up neatly outside the door. Tamar wondered how they could all tell their identical shoes apart. She decided to write her name in hers.

The desks were all lined up in groups of two, facing one end of the room. The boys sat on one side, the girls on the other. Tamar sat with Pat.

Soon the first teacher came in. They all *wai*-ed and *sawatdee*-ed, and then the teacher beckoned to Tamar, led her into the corridor, and pointed to an office at the end of the hall. Tamar put her shoes back on and went there.

She knocked on the door, heard a heavily accented voice say, "Come in" in English, and did so. A man sat at a desk. He had a red, bulbous nose. She *wai*-ed and *sawatdee*-ed. He gave her a half-hearted return *wai*, smiled and said, "Sit down," so she did.

"You are Arisa," he said, and she nodded. "I am Ajahn Prichawat. Welcome to our school."

"Thank you."

"I am an English teacher, and I am your advisor. You do not speak Thai yet."

"Only a little."

"Yes, so I think you can have classes like art, dance, sewing, so you can learn by seeing and doing and you do not have to speak."

"That sounds like a good idea."

"This means you will be with many different classes, not with your sister's class all the time, maybe some much younger classes."

"That's okay."

"Okay. I made a schedule." He said it in the British way: sheh-jool. He handed her a piece of paper. "The rooms are easy to find. Do you know Thai numbers?"

"Sort of."

"The rooms have English numbers too, so it doesn't matter. Ajahn Sumalee, another English teacher, will teach you Thai class in the library, Tuesday and Thursday at 2p.m. You can see on the schedule. Okay?"

"Okay."

"Okay. What class do you have now?"

"I'm not sure what this says." She showed the paper to Ajahn Prichawat.

"Swordfighting."

"Swordfighting?"

"Yes. Thai swordfighting. Not dangerous. It is a kind of dancing." He looked at her unconvinced face and laughed.

"You will have fun. You can just watch, Room 122."

Tamar made her way down to Room 122. It was a large, high-ceilinged room, filled with 12 year olds who all started whispering when she came in. They were all in P.E. uniforms, sweatpants and big, loose, collared shirts, like golf shirts, but of a thicker, smoother material, and all dark blue. A couple of the boys shouted "Hello." She said hello back, and made the girls giggle. One particularly mischievous boy walked up to her with his hand out, ready for shaking. She didn't fall for that one, though. She had learned at Camp that boys and girls weren't supposed to touch each other, and that shaking a boy's hand would be very risqué. Instead, she gave him a very low I-am-superior-to-you *wai* and said *sawatdee*.

The whole room started bubbling with giggles and a sound like "Oho!" with a very long final "o". The boy retreated into his ridiculing group of friends. The teacher walked in and silence was immediate. He was compact and stood very straight. He walked smoothly over to her and she *wai*-ed as politely as she could. He asked her a question, the only word of which she understood being "you." She showed him her schedule and pointed to Room 122. He nodded and pointed to a place near the wall from which, she gathered, she could watch the class.

They used "swords" made from metal tubes, about half an inch in diameter, with handles and rounded ends. They followed the teacher in routines that really were like dancing: standing, sitting, kneeling, whirling around, swords flipping back and forth, slashing and stabbing the air, fierce looks on their previously giggling faces. It was beautiful, and impressive, and when the class was over, she wanted very much to tell the teacher so, but she didn't have the words. He may have been able to read it in her face, though, because he smiled, and, with a mix of words, some of which she understood, and gestures, such as pointing to the dressing area and the other students' clothes, indicated that next time she should come dressed to participate. She *wai*-ed and said "*kopkun mahk-ka*" and he nodded.

She checked her schedule and saw that her next class was Thai music. This was going to be so much better than going to school back home.

Chapter 9

Aside from Thai lessons, which seemed to be more about Ajahn Sumalee's improving her English than Tamar's improving her Thai, all of her classes were enjoyable. She learned more about Thai culture every day. The teachers were used to more deference than she was used to giving, but she wanted to be as Thai as possible, so she *wai*-ed and kept her head low.

One day, though, during a rainstorm, she decided to alter her decision, at least in one case. When it rained, they lined up in the corridors for morning *kaotao*, instead of outside.

She was standing in line with Pat's class, facing out the window, when the computer teacher Ajahn Aroon, whose office was down the hall, came walking by. He stopped behind her, leaned over her shoulder, and, reeking of alcohol, said something she didn't quite understand. It seemed to be an attempt at English. She caught "dream" and "you". She turned around, and the leer on his face made his meaning clear enough. All her learned Thai deference escaped her and the derisive sneer of the disgusted American teenager formed itself on her face. His expression didn't change, but he walked away.

When she told Ajahn Prichawat, he said, "Don't worry about it. He will not hurt you. *Mai pellai*." Clearly, she was on her own. So, she resolved never again to show Ajahn Aroon any respect. She managed mostly to stay away from him, but when she did pass him in the halls, she stood up perfectly straight, looked him directly in the eyes, and kept her hands at her sides. She expected to be reprimanded at any moment, but she didn't care what the custom was. She was willing to bow her head and *wai* politely to people she didn't truly respect, but not someone she found both physically and morally repulsive. There was something in her that had a limit, and this was it.

She was prepared to accept punishment for her show of disrespect. Oddly enough, though, punishment never came. Everyone ignored her disrespect of Ajahn Aroon the same way she was expected to ignore his drunken leers. He never again got close to her, and soon her not *wai*-ing him became less a defiant act and more a habit.

Another rainy day, she was with Pat's class, stuck in their classroom for the equivalent of recess. Pat and the other girls were talking and giggling on one side of the room, and the boys were on the other. She listened to the girls' conversation for a while, trying to pick up new words, but, from what she could understand, the main topic of discussion seemed to be the Hello Kitty line of change purses and figurines, and how cute they were. Since Tamar had found this topic boring even in elementary school, she soon found it difficult to concentrate. Her eyes wandered over to the boys, gathered around a few desks they had pushed together.

Many of the boys had their arms around each other. She had been very surprised when she first saw boys walking around holding hands with their friends, or with their arms around each other's waists, just like the girls did. Once she got used to it, she started to feel sorry for American boys, unable to show that kind of affection for their friends. This seemed much more sensible, much more egalitarian.

She saw that the boys had a checkerboard on the desks. She moved closer, trying to determine if the game they were playing was the same game she had played at home so many times. Some of the boys saw her looking, and made space for her to get closer. It turned out to be exactly the same checkers game she knew. She hadn't played in years, but seeing the familiar jumping and kinging was exciting.

Soon that match was over, and the next one underway. Tamar watched and cheered, albeit quietly, with the crowd. When that game ended, the boys motioned for her to take the loser's seat. They all moved out of the way so she could get to it without touching any of them. The familiarity drew her in, and she agreed. The boys seemed excited about her participation, until she started to win. When she jumped the last checker, she got no cheers at all. She couldn't understand the words the boys said, but they were directed toward her opponent, and were clearly ridicule. She decided not to take on another challenger, and just as she got up, the bell rang, so she rushed downstairs to Thai Art.

At home that evening, no one would speak to her. Pat, PiJai, even Nong just ignored her if she spoke to them. She grabbed some fruit for dinner and went to bed early. The next day it was the same, and all the girls in Pat's class ignored her the same way. She knew she must have done something to offend them. She thought it might have been playing checkers with the boys. She wasn't sure, though. She hadn't touched any of them, and she knew she was allowed to talk to them. The boys and girls joked together often at school. She didn't get it, and she didn't know how to fix it.

On the third day, she cornered PiJai alone in the bedroom. With desperation in her voice she said, "PiJai, *deechun ngong mahk*. I'm very confused. Obviously I did something wrong, but I don't know what, and whatever it was, I didn't mean to do it."

PiJai kept reading.

"PiJai, please tell me. I just want to fix it. Was it playing checkers the other day? Should I not have done that?"

PiJai put her book down. "You should know that. You have been here long enough. You know boys and girls should stay separate."

"I know that, but I guess I don't really know how separate they should be. I know I'm not supposed to touch them. I don't shake hands or anything, but the girls and boys talk together at school. They joke together. I didn't realize. Really, I wouldn't have done it if I had known. They were so polite about it. They didn't act as if I was doing anything bad."

"You know they will try to trick you, like shaking hands."

"You're right. I should have figured it out. I'm really sorry. I didn't understand what the girls were talking about, and… I just didn't think. I'm really sorry. What can I do? Should I apologize?"

"No, you will only make it worse. Better not to talk about it. Just be nice to Chang, and stay with the girls from now on."

"I will. I promise. I'm really sorry."

"Okay. *Mai pellai.*"

"*Kopkun-ka.*"

PiJai went back to her book. Tamar stuck close to Pat and her friends the next day, even though they weren't speaking to her, and didn't even look at the boys. That night at dinner, Pat put some food on her plate and asked if it was good. The day after that, it was suddenly as if nothing had happened. The girls were friendly and smiling, trying to include her in their conversations. The transformation was so complete that Tamar briefly wondered if the whole checkers incident was just a nightmare she'd had, or a bizarre daydream, but the next stormy day, the boys brought out the board again, and Tamar focused as intensely as she could on the cuteness of Hello Kitty.

Soon after that, Tamar had to take a test. She was far enough ahead at school back home that she had very few academic requirements for her year away, but she did have to read a few books, write a few essays, and take the Advanced Placement English exam. She was to take it in the morning, and then attend her classes in the afternoon.

PiTey drove her to the International School, which had high white walls and a wrought-iron gate, like her house, but as she walked across the schoolyard, looking for Room 163, she became increasingly self-conscious. The International School may as well have been the American School. She heard nothing but American English. The girls were wearing halter tops, shorts, high heels and makeup. The boys had long hair and jeans, and everyone seemed to be smoking.

She felt like a foreigner, a hick and a prude, in her little-girl uniform and maryjanes, with her bare face and unshaved legs. Everyone stared at her as she walked by. The strangest thing was, though, that her first thought, on seeing those students, who would have looked ordinary at any U.S. high school, was not "Oh look. Here are people like me," but, "what a bunch of tramps and degenerates." It shocked her, that thought, coming from her own mind. Had she absorbed such a different point of view in just a few months? She decided not to think about it. She had to focus on the test.

The test wasn't bad at all. It was just a couple of essays. One of them was about <u>Catcher in the Rye</u>, which she loved. It was almost fun, but she was still glad when it was over.

When she came out of room 163, the schoolyard was empty. Everyone was in class. As she walked out the gate, she heard the bell ring for lunch. She was glad to have escaped their stares on the way out. She had gotten used to being stared at by Thais as she walked around in her school uniform, with her pale skin and red hair, but this was a different kind of stare, or rather, the same kind of stare from the opposite direction. What was a white girl doing in a Thai school uniform?

She got on the bus and headed to her regular school. A woman standing near her was asking another woman how many stops until Central Plaza. Tamar realized that, not only did she understand the entire conversation, but she also knew the answer to the question and, even more, how to say it, so she did. The woman understood her, thanked her, and got off at the right stop. Tamar thought, let them wonder about me, and let them stare. I can speak Thai.

The trip from her house to the FSA office was now an easy one. By the fourth rehearsal, PiEng finally seemed happy with their grasp of the Thai folk dance. It was a good thing, because the dance was to be performed in just another week. It was for some sort of Thai-American conference, and the U.S. ambassador and some other American diplomats were going to be there.

The night of the dance, they were dressed up in brightly colored costumes. PiEng put bright makeup on them, even the boys, and sprayed their hair up. They were all very nervous, but they remembered the steps. Joel dropped his net once, but he picked it up and didn't miss a step.

When they were done, they were directed over to the dais where the ambassador had commemorative gifts to hand out to them. They hadn't been told about that part. They all *wai*-ed as they received their gifts. Photos were snapped as they did so.

Tamar felt something like a fog over her brain the whole time. She had a vague awareness of a large audience, several hundred people at least, sitting at round tables far below the stage. She performed her steps with a big smile on her face, but in a kind of haze, not thinking about the steps, not thinking at all. She noticed when Joel dropped his net, but it didn't affect her in any way. When it was all over and she walked outside, she felt a sensation like waking up from an unintentional nap, a return to a reality she hadn't known she had left.

On the ride home, PiLahng asked, "Why did you *wai* and say *kopkun*? Why didn't you shake hands and say thank you?"

They all looked at each other, surprised by the question. Tamar said, "I don't know. I didn't think about it."

Ben said, "It just seemed natural."

"But the American ambassador is not Thai," said PiLahng.

"Yeah," Joel said, "but we are." They all looked at Joel. "Sort of."

PiLahng still looked puzzled.

Ciara said, "Besides, Tamar and I can't shake the ambassador's hand. He's a boy." They started laughing.

"Right. Ooh, you're too close to me. You boys better stay on that side of the van."

"Cooties! Cooties!"

"Get away!"

"Enough! Enough!" said PiLahng.

That quieted them for a moment, but then Ciara said, very quietly, "Well, maybe we're not completely Thai." They couldn't stop laughing.

Chapter 10

One Friday afternoon, Pat invited Tamar to *bpai tee-oh* (go out to have fun) with her and her friends. Tamar thought it might actually be fun, because now she could understand most of what they said, and even join in the conversation a little.

They met at Dtom's house, and the girls seemed even gigglier than usual. When Tamar asked where they were going, they said *bpai Dunkin*, which was not much of a surprise. When they were on the bus, they giggled even more, and she asked what was going on. They didn't want to say, but then Dtom let slip something about a "*fan*", a boyfriend. Tamar was very surprised. She hadn't thought any of them had boyfriends. She asked "*Krai mee fan*, who's got a boyfriend?" and they all looked at Ang. So, they were going to Dunkin' Donuts to see Ang's boyfriend.

When they arrived, some boys from school were already there, sitting at a table. The girls did not join them, but walked over to a nearby table, giggling all the way. The boys were giggling almost as much as the girls.

Just after Dtom brought their donuts to the table, one of the boys got up and headed in their direction. Tamar thought he must be Ang's *fan*, but then he just handed a note to Pat and went back to the other table. Pat gave the note to Ang. She opened it and blushed. Even Tamar could read what it said: *Ang suay mahk* (Ang is very beautiful). The girls made ooh noises and giggled some more. Then Ang gave Pat a note, which she brought to the boys' table. They passed it to the boy who must really be the *fan*. He opened and read it and they giggled. Then he gave a small package to one of the other boys to pass to the girls, to pass to Ang. It was a Hello Kitty changepurse.

A few days later, Ciara invited Tamar to go shopping, and PiJai let her go. As they walked through the market, she told the whole romantic story. "That was the date," Tamar said. "Sitting there at different tables passing notes. It was like third grade or something. First grade. Kindergarten."

"My host sister has a *fan*. He comes to dinner sometimes, and they don't even talk."

"I don't get it. PiJai said that it's really serious, too, that once you have a *fan* you're supposed to marry him, eventually, stay together all through college and grad school, and then get married, but I don't know how you can choose someone if you don't even speak."

"Maybe it's an arranged thing."

"Maybe. Oh shoot. The rain is early."

Vendors rushed to cover their merchandise. The girls rushed to the street. They both had the same idea: Central Plaza. It was only a few blocks away, and completely protected from the rain. They got as far as across the street, and then hit an obstacle. The main road was completely flooded. A *dtukdtuk* floated by without a driver. The water looked several feet deep.

"We could wade it. There aren't any cars coming." Ciara said. Tamar looked at the brown water, trash floating in it. She thought of all the disgusting things that might be hidden in the murk. Then she thought, I'm here for adventure, and stepped in.

It was as disgusting as she had imagined, slimy, smelly and cold. In some places, the water was as high as her hip, although it mostly splashed about her knees. When they got to the other side, they were glad it was still pouring hard. They walked slowly toward the nearest entrance to Central Plaza, letting the rain wash off some of the muck.

When they went inside, they started shuddering. They had forgotten about the full blast air-conditioning. They looked at each other, and went back outside. They found a covered bus stop to stand under, and watched the debris float down the street.

"I knew the curbs were high here, but I didn't realize they were that much higher than the middle of the street." Said Tamar. "Now we know why."

"Yeah. It must have been pretty before they filled in all the canals."

"I read they used to call Bangkok the Venice of the East."

"We should go to the floating market sometime. I guess that's sort of what it used to be like."

"Yeah."

The rain let up, and the sun came out, and everything started to dry. They walked to the other side of Central Plaza and caught a *dtukdtuk* to Ciara's house.

The family compound was huge. Aside from the four houses, there were several other buildings, including a garage and what looked like it might be servants' quarters. The buildings were spread out over an entire city block, surrounded by a wall. They walked through an iron gate and over to the largest of the houses. The front door was dark, heavy and decorated with carved dragons. It opened onto a hallway with a long staircase and a very high ceiling. Ciara led the way up the stairs. She had her own room, next door to her host sister Ing's, and her own bathroom. They cleaned up a bit, and sat on the floor to talk.

"This is a great house. Is this the first wife's?"

"Yeah. KoonPaw is here a lot, too."

"You call him KoonPaw? I guess he's really Thai then. My host father is Papa, but that may be a Chinese thing. I think he and Mama came from Hong Kong. So your host mother is KoonMeh?"

"Mm hm. Yeah, they're really Thai. I think the family has been here at this same spot for a long time."

"Old money."

"Yeah, I think so."

"Justine told me she read somewhere that polygamy is illegal in Thailand."

"An *ajahn* at school told me that they don't really marry them all. They marry the first one, but the rest just live there and everyone calls them wives."

"That's a weird thing. I don't get how they work it out."

"I don't think they see each other much. I mean, I've never been in the other houses."

"Papa's wives all live in the same house. I snuck upstairs once. There are three bedrooms, but I don't know which one Papa sleeps in."

"Maybe he rotates."

They both started laughing.

"I guess I shouldn't make fun of it. I mean, my dad's had a lot of wives too, just not at the same time."

"That's different, though."

"I know. I'm just trying to be fair, or to find something to compare it to, or something. I mean, it's weird."

"Definitely weird, but normal too, you know, because it's normal for them."

"Yeah. They don't seem to mind."

They both stared at the walls for a moment. Then Tamar said, "Your parents are still married, right?"

"Mm hm."

"I don't think I know anyone, back home, whose parents are still married. There's this one girl at school. No, wait. I guess there are a few people."

"I know a lot of people."

"I guess they stay married longer in Columbus than they do in L.A."

"Does it bother you? I mean, do you wish they'd stayed married."

"No, I don't wish that. I mean, I think they're both better off, but I kind of wish they wouldn't keep getting married and then divorced and then married and then divorced, especially my dad. My mom's been married to David for six years now, and they seem really happy. They have Sam and Noah and it's this great family, but you never know. I mean, it's the third marriage for both of them. He's got other kids from before, and she's got me. Then my dad, he's about to get married for the fifth time, and each one has only lasted four or five years. I want to be excited for him, but I think I'd rather wait five years or so. You know? It just gets to be a lot."

"So, how many brothers and sisters do you have?"

"Well, it depends how you count. As far as actually related to me, there are Sam and Noah with my mom, and then Amy and Heather and Melissa and Ryan on my dad's side, so that's six half-siblings, but there are all the steps and the sort of step steps."

"What are step steps?"

"I don't think it's really a word, but like David's oldest daughters, Pat and Liz, their mom is remarried and they have kids, and I see them pretty often, so Pat and Liz are my stepsisters, but the others really aren't, but they have to be something. I mean they are sort of family."

"Wow."

"And like my mom's second husband, he has six sons, so for a while they were my stepbrothers, but they're not anymore, and I don't really ever see them, so are they family or not? They're sort of ex-family I guess."

"That is way too complicated."

"Exactly. Maybe four wives in four houses is really simpler."

They both stared at the ceiling for a while. Then Ciara said, "Let's go see if they're putting dinner out yet."

The table in the dining room had a marble top, and servants were busy filling it up with food, the bowls and platters clinking on the stone. Ciara's host sister walked in the room and greeted them. Tamar had trouble understanding Ciara's family when they spoke because they used more formal vocabulary and less slang than hers, but she understood when Ing asked if she would like to stay for dinner, and perhaps spend the night. She called home to see if she could, and was happy to hear PiJai's voice, until she said, sternly, "I think you should come home for dinner."

Ing offered to have their driver take her, but Tamar thought that was too much hospitality, and she liked taking the bus. It made her feel so competent. She liked the surprised looks on people's faces when she spoke Thai to the conductor. She wondered if she was in trouble, if she'd done something wrong again, but it didn't seem that way. Maybe good Thai girls were always home for dinner.

Chapter 11

Tamar's eating seemed to be a very important subject. Everyone was always handing her food. At first, she had tried it all, but now she was worried about getting fat. Her school uniform skirts were getting tight.

One night, Papa brought home a whole tray of sweets from the food factory he owned, new products for them all to try. She was still full the next day, and had just a small serving of vegetables for lunch at school. That afternoon, Ajahn Prichawat called her into his office.

"You are not eating properly," he said. "You must eat, or you will get sick."

"I just wasn't hungry today," she said.

"You must eat. You must stay very healthy. Your host family will be ashamed to send you home skinny and sickly."

"But I'm not skinny or sickly, and normally I eat plenty. I just ate a lot yesterday, so I'm not hungry today."

Ajahn's face became very red. He very nearly raised his voice. "You are not a camel!" he said. "You must eat lunch!"

"Okay. Tomorrow, I promise to eat lunch."

"Good."

She called Ciara that night.

"I feel like a turkey in November," said Tamar.

"They're all trying to get us fat. I talked to Noelle and she said she'd gained five kilos."

"Well, I'm sure I've gained a few pounds, but I'm not gaining any more. I'm not going to let them stuff me anymore."

"Good luck. It's some sort of status thing, I think. It shows they're rich and they feed us well."

"Well, too bad. I have to eat a decent lunch, though. Ajahn Prichawat must have spies."

She tried to get exercise when she could, but then one day in August she sprained her ankle going down the stairs. She stayed home from school for a week.

On Wednesday, she was reading on PiJai's bed, when Pat and Nong came rushing in. They tried to tell her something had happened, but she couldn't understand the words. Pat got her Thai-English dictionary and looked something up. She showed Tamar the page, and pointed to the word "revolution." That made no sense at all to Tamar. On Mondays, the older boys came to school in green uniforms and did ROTC type exercises in the main courtyard. She thought maybe they were describing some kind of war games, but they kept insisting on that word, revolution.

They were still trying to explain it to her when PiJai came home. "PiJai! *Mai kao jai*. I don't understand at all. They keep saying revolution."

"Yes. Some soldiers attacked the government."

"What?"

"They have big guns downtown."

"What? You mean somebody is trying to take over the government? Like a military coup?"

"Yes! Coup. That's the word. A military coup."

"You mean there's a coup happening right now?"

"Yes. Maybe. Attempted coup. It happens every four or five years."

"You mean there are soldiers out there right now?"

"Not here. Only downtown. It is safe. You don't have to worry."

Tamar couldn't understand PiJai's calm. At least Pat and Nong showed some concern. Every four or five years? She thought about saying, "In the U.S., we have elections," but that seemed much too rude, so she just stared at PiJai.

There was no sign of turmoil right there at the house. The weather was as hot as usual. There were no strange sounds, no booming guns or yelling crowds. Flashes of movies and newsclips went through Tamar's mind, desperate, screaming people climbing fences, running for helicopters. Maybe her parents had been right to worry about her.

PiJai didn't seem to think so, though, and Pat and Nong were calmer now too. Maybe it really was possible that an attempted coup was no real crisis at all, just something that happens every few years, like a decent sized earthquake in L.A. She decided to trust PiJai. She didn't have a better idea, anyway.

By the next day it was over. There was a picture on the front page of the morning paper of a tank in front of one of the government buildings. Everyone went to work and school as usual.

Her mother called from L.A., and she pretended she had never been afraid, that it was absolutely nothing at all. She didn't want to cause worry, but even more she didn't want to provide an excuse for an early return home. She stayed perfectly calm, asked how David and the boys were doing, and was apparently convincing, because her mother brought up the idea of her flying home only once.

Ciara said her host family hadn't discussed the coup at all. She only heard about it at school, where there was a rumor that one school, close to the action, had been evacuated.

Tamar found herself wishing she had been at that school, just for the excitement of it, the adventure. Then she told herself that was a ridiculous thing to wish, and she should be happy to have been stuck at home with a sprained ankle, where her mother wouldn't have to worry about her, but she still wished it.

The situation made her feel bold somehow, and she took the opportunity to ask PiJai what she knew would be a sensitive question. She had figured out that Nong's name was short for *nong sao*, little sister, and she could see that Nong's position in the house was a little odd. She went to a less prestigious school. She sometimes helped the servants with their chores. She clearly was not on the same footing in the household as PiJai and Pat.

The next time Tamar found PiJai alone, doing some work on her drafting board, she plunged right in. "PiJai," she said, "I've been wondering about Nong."

PiJai tensed, but Tamar continued. "I mean, is she actually your sister?"

"Yes. Nong is my sister."

"But Mama isn't her mother, right? Who is her mother?"

PiJai got up and walked straight into the bathroom. Just before she closed and locked the door, she said, "Nong's mother left a long time ago, fifteen years ago."

Tamar stood staring at the bathroom door. So, there was another woman, maybe another wife, and she left her baby daughter. Tamar was happy PiJai had told her that much. She decided it was better not to press for details.

So, PiJai and Pat had Mama to look out for them, and Djoh and Djim had Meh, but Nong had to take care of herself. She didn't even have a full brother or sister.

"*Kopkun-ka*, PiJai," Tamar said through the door, and then she went downstairs.

Chapter 12

With September came the Mid-Year Camp. FSA was taking them all to a beach resort at Pang Nga. Tamar danced around the room with her walkman as she packed.

PiTey drove her to the FSA office, where two schoolbuses were waiting, already mostly filled. The laughter subsided as she arrived, and for every arrival after her, while everyone looked to see who it was. Recognition was followed by shrieks and hugs.

Tamar sat with Ben and Duncan and Selena and Fransje. Ciara was on the other bus with Rowena and Nerissa. Another car drove up and released a tall, skinny blonde.

"Who's that?" someone said.

"I've never seen her before."

"Maybe there's a new student."

They all stared as PiLahng greeted the strange girl and led her into the office. A little while later, Noelle came out and got on the bus.

"Did you see Anne?" she asked. No one had. "She just walked into the office a few minutes ago with PiLahng."

"That was Anne?"

"Yeah. She's lost nearly 20 kilos in six months. She says she doesn't like Thai food. She eats nothing but fruit, and not much of that. They're sending her home. They say she's anorexic."

"Jack went home too," said Justine. "Last month. He didn't get along very well with his host family, and he just got too homesick, so he left."

"I heard eleven people have switched families, because they didn't get along."

"I heard Rowena's switched three times already."

All the way through Bangkok, the conversation was about who was on the verge of being kicked out of school, or even sent home, whose family refused to speak Thai with them, because they wanted their children to learn English, who was a virtual prisoner, not allowed out without a chaperone, and who snuck out every night to party.

Tamar hadn't heard any of this before. She had thought Jack seemed unhappy, but she hadn't considered the possibility that someone would just decide to go home. She had barely known Anne, but she thought something must have gone terribly wrong with her, but then again maybe she really just did not like Thai food.

When they left Bangkok and headed down the road south, they picked up speed, and a breeze blew through the windows. Everyone stopped talking to enjoy it. They were out of the city, heading for the beach. Duncan and Selena got out their guitars and started to play.

The resort at Pang Nga turned out to be a bunch of very rustic shacks with bunkbeds, and huge locker room-like bathrooms with Thai toilets and a huge tank of water instead of a shower, but the beach was postcard beautiful, with pale yellow sand and rock formations around the edges, and water that couldn't quite decide if it was clear blue or deep green, and it was a private beach, so the girls would be able to wear real bathing suits, and not have to be covered up in T-shirts and Bermuda shorts.

Tamar was assigned to a cabin with Fransje and Noelle and Selena. She grabbed a top bunk. The resident spider in the corner barely bothered her. The first thing they did was throw on their suits and go in the water, except for Selena. She said she might join them later.

The water was beautifully cool, and clear to the bottom. There were barely any waves, but Tamar and Noelle taught Fransje how to bodysurf anyway. They stayed in the water until a gong called them to dinner. When they came back to their cabin to change, Selena was still there, sitting on a lower bunk, playing her guitar.

That night, Rowena led a group sneaking into town to find a bar. Tamar stayed with a group that sat on the beach and watched the waves while they sang along with Duncan and Selena. She liked that the Aussies and Kiwis knew all the same campfire songs she did, although she got in an argument with Duncan about the pronunciation of Jim Croce's last name. He kept insisting it was "crochet". He knew all his best songs, though.

Noelle was completely enamored of Duncan, staring at him all the time, finding any excuse to get close. In fact, many of the girls seemed to have crushes on him. Tamar thought he was cute, and sweet, and fun, but he was such a hippie surfer, and she knew so many hippie surfers back home. She found Ben much more exotic, with his stories of running through the cornfields of Nebraska, where his father was a minister, and absolutely everybody went to church absolutely every Sunday, and people said "goobers" and "darn it" and then apologized for their bad language. She didn't really believe that existed anywhere except on 1950s TV shows, but Ben was entertaining, once he got past his initial shyness, and she liked hearing his stories, even if she didn't quite believe them.

Joel was generally happy too, and outspoken and fun. She liked Duncan well enough too, and Antony from New Zealand was very cute.

She guessed she had mini-crushes on all of them, but she wasn't head-over-heels for any of them. Poor Noelle. Duncan didn't seem to notice.

She went to sleep to the sound of the waves and the feel of the breeze. She thought, I'll remember this as the high point of the whole year.

The next day they were piled into a couple of boats for a water tour. The high point was supposed to be the island where Dr. No, the James Bond movie, was filmed. It was actually the most unimpressive place they visited, just a little island with a stretch of beach between some mossy rock formations. Many of the other islands were much more beautiful.

The most interesting part for Tamar was the Muslim village on stilts. She didn't know why it was pointed out that it was a Muslim village. There weren't any Buddhas or incense, but there weren't any minarets either. What was interesting was that there was no land at all. All the buildings were on stilts in the water, connected by boardwalks. It was beautiful on this sunny day, with the water lapping at the pilings, but it didn't look sturdy enough to withstand a big storm. They didn't stay there long.

Tamar didn't see Ciara much. She waved and said hi if they passed, but she didn't much like being around Rowena and the party girls, and she definitely didn't want to get involved in whatever they were doing in town at night.

She could understand a little, though, their wanting to ignore all the Thai restrictions. It was nice to be able to wear what she wanted, and to hang out late into the night, boys and girls together, perfectly innocently, as friends. As she fell asleep, she wondered if anyone had a checkerboard.

The next morning, most of the girls were in the *hong nam*, brushing their teeth, washing their hair. Tamar was in her sarong, like most of the others, rinsing soap off herself with water from the tank, when Selena, who was on the opposite side of the tank, splashed Noelle, who was next to her. Noelle told her not to, and she did it again, with more water. Then she threw a bowlful toward Fransje, who was on the other side of her, a bit farther away. Fransje told her to stop. Everyone's attention was on Selena now.

She started splashing randomly, scooping up bowls of water and throwing them in all directions. She was laughing, too, although no one else was. It was as if she thought she was in the middle of a *Songkran* water fight. She kept flinging water and getting more and more people annoyed with her.

Then she started running around the tank, laughing and waving a plastic bowl around. She'd stop to scoop up some water from the tank, then go back to running. Her laughing started sounding more like screaming. She was just running around the bathroom, shrieking and splashing.

Tamar's feet would not move, and she couldn't stop staring. Most of the other girls had the same reaction. Someone with a better grasp of the situation ran out and got PiLahng. By the time she got there, with a couple of FSA volunteers, Selena's sarong had fallen off, and she was running around naked, shrieking, still with a plastic bowl in her hand. The adults grabbed her by the arms, wrapped her in a towel, and took her outside.

Tamar and the others stood in the bathroom and looked at each other. No one said anything more coherent than, "Oh my God." After a few minutes, they all, as if by subconscious mutual agreement, went back to brushing their teeth and washing their hair, but silently. Then they walked to the dining hall, silently. There, though, conversation began again, because the boys, and the girls who had slept late, like Ciara and her friends, all wanted to know what had happened.

Ciara and Rowena sat down next to Tamar and Noelle. Rowena said, "So what happened in there, girls? I heard screaming. I thought someone was being tortured to death. Was somebody beating poor Selena with her guitar." She let out just a small laugh.

Ciara smiled faintly. Noelle just looked down at her food. Tamar said, in an absolutely level, humorless voice. "I don't know what happened. I've never seen anything like that before in my life. I don't think I've even seen anything like that in the movies. It was the strangest thing I ever saw."

"But what did she do?" Ciara asked.

"She was just standing there at the tank, washing off like everyone else, and she started splashing people. She splashed Noelle first."

They all looked at Noelle, who kept her head down. Rowena nudged her, "so you started it all, eh?"

Before Tamar could open her mouth, Ciara said, "Rowena, stop it."

Rowena rolled her eyes.

"So she just started splashing people?" asked Ciara.

"Yeah, and everyone told her to stop, but she wouldn't, and then she started running around the tank and screaming, and then PiLahng came and they took her away. It was really fast. She was just standing there, like everyone else, and then she was splashing and running and screaming. It was so weird. I didn't think it happened like that, in real life, that people just sort of snap like that."

"So you don't know what set her off?"

"Nothing set her off. She just went off, completely out of nowhere."

"Well, they've locked her up now." Said Rowena.

Tamar was startled. Noelle looked up. Her eyes were wet. Tamar turned to Ciara. "Is that true?"

"I don't know. We heard they were taking her to a mental hospital."

Tamar thought about what a Thai mental hospital might be like. She couldn't get a clear picture, but she had a general impression of bars and bugs, and people screaming, like Selena did.

Rowena leaned toward Noelle. "You sure you didn't have anything to do with it?"

"Hey!" Tamar was getting annoyed. "Leave her alone!"

Rowena got up. "I need a ciggy anyway," she said as she left the room.

"Rowena's being an idiot," Tamar told Noelle. "You know it had nothing to do with you. You were just there, like the rest of us."

"Right. I know. It's just hard to think about. I've never seen anything like that."

"Me neither. She'll be okay. She just freaked out. She'll be fine."

"Yeah."

They ate the rest of their breakfast in silence.

Later that morning, Tamar found Duncan sitting under a tree with his guitar, not really playing anything, just picking at it. She sat down in front of him. "You were there, yeah?" he said.

She nodded.

"I tried to go with her to hospital, but they wouldn't let me."

She nodded again.

"I've been learning so much from her. She's a great musician. Much better than I am."

"She has a beautiful voice too."

"Yeah. They're taking her someplace near here. PiLahng said I might be able to visit her in a couple of weeks."

"Good."

"Yeah." He kept picking at his guitar, and she dug at the sand with her toes until lunchtime.

After dinner that night, Tamar went to her room to get her copy of The Great Gatsby for Ben, who had never read it. On her way back to the beach, it was very quiet. She heard nothing but the waves and a couple of birds. Then, as she turned a corner, there was Ciara, also alone. "Hi." Tamar said, startled.

"Hi" Ciara said.

"You're not going into town tonight?"

"I'm kind of tired."

"Oh."

"That was weird, what happened today."

"Yeah. She'll be okay, though."

"Yeah. I hope so." They both looked down at their feet. Tamar was about to say goodbye and walk on when Ciara said, "Hey, Tamar, you're not mad at me or anything, right?"

"No. Why would you think that?"

"I don't know. I mean, it's been a weird day and everything. It's just we haven't talked much and sometimes it seems kind of…"

"No. The reason I don't come talk to you is that you're always with Rowena and those girls and I don't want to interrupt or bug you."

"And you're with Noelle and Ben and those guys and I don't want to come over there."

They looked at each other for a moment, and then Ciara said, "So why are we friends anyway?"

Tamar smiled. "I have no idea."

"Are you busy right now?"

"Not really."

"You want to go down by the water?"

"Yeah."

They sat close enough to watch the waves but far enough to stay dry.

"Do you think we'll be different, when we go home?" asked Ciara.

"I think so. I think maybe we already are different."

"Really? How?"

"I don't know. Some people are having a really hard time here. I like it, but some of it is hard. I mean, some of the customs and stuff. You get sort of used to it, but you change in the process, I think. When I went to the International School for that test, it was so weird, to be around all those Americans, acting like they were in America, like nothing was different at all."

"I guess for them it's not. I mean, they probably don't even talk to Thai people."

"They probably don't even speak Thai."

"Maybe we won't really be different, though. We're still Americans."

"Yeah, we'll always be Americans, but maybe we'll understand more what that means, you know, because we really have something to compare it to now."

"We definitely have something to compare it to, and it definitely is different."

"Yeah."

That night Tamar thought about Selena, and Anne, and Jack who went home. She thought about what is was like talking with Ciara, almost like with a sister, maybe exactly like that. She didn't have a real sister, just stepsisters, and half-sisters she rarely saw, so she wasn't sure. She wondered why people acted the ways they did. She thought maybe there was such a thing as fate, or maybe weird things just happened, all the time. For some reason, she started thinking about her Thai swordfighting class. She fell asleep without figuring anything out.

Chapter 13

A few days later, when they went back to Bangkok, Ciara and Rowena ended up on the same bus with Tamar. There was a conspiratorial air on the bus. Some of the people who lived out in the country were staying with friends in Bangkok for a few days. A few others would have one night at a hotel, catching trains and buses the next day. They were discussing what to do that night. The boys, of course, wanted to go to *Patpong*.

Patpong was the famous Bangkok red light district. Some of the boys had been there before, and insisted that it was more than just a bunch of prostitutes, that there were really interesting shows, lots of dancing. Rowena said she had been too, and they should all see it once. "Loads of *sanuk* (fun), and you can tell your friends when you go back home."

Ciara was going, and Joel, and Duncan and Fransje. Tamar had never considered going there, but she was curious. She wanted to see what it was like. She knew her parents wouldn't want her to go, but they were on the other side of the world. It didn't sound so dangerous, and she'd be with people who had been there before. She decided to go.

She wasn't sure how to manage the logistics, though. Her host family knew she was supposed to be home that day. She decided to try asking for permission to spend the night at Ciara's house.

She hadn't much hope, since PiJai hadn't let her even stay there for dinner, but she would try.

She was lucky. The only one home seemed to be PiSey. Tamar tried to explain in Thai that she would be arriving in Bangkok late, so, since Ciara's house was near the FSA office, where the bus would drop them off, it seemed smarter to stay there and come home in the morning, rather than brave the buses at night. She figured that the message would be somewhat confused, but the basic idea, that she was somewhere for the night and would come home in the morning, would get through. She might get in trouble, but she had decided to do this thing. She wasn't sure why. Maybe she wasn't as different from Rowena and the party girls as she thought she was.

She didn't dress up for the occasion. She didn't want to make a big deal out of it, and the only clothes she had with her were the ones she brought to camp, anyway. She let Ciara put makeup on her, though, just a little. She wouldn't let Rowena do it.

There were twelve of them. They went in two *dtukdtuks*, sitting on each other's laps. Tamar expected to feel something ominous approaching, or to see some change in the night landscape, something dangerous, but it really didn't seem different from going shopping. They rattled through the traffic as usual. The only difference was that it was dark out.

When they arrived, Tamar was surprised, almost stunned, at how innocuous it looked. *Patpong* was like some sort of parallel universe Disneyland exhibit: Sex Industry Land. It was just a few blocks long, and very crowded, with lights everywhere, strung across the street like for a parade, music coming out of every door, obvious tourists gawking. Heavily made up, scantily clad women moved through the crowd, saying hello to wealthy-looking men, or rather, relatively wealthy-looking, those who looked like they had at least twenty bucks, and trying to lure them into the bars. It was all so blatant, though. Tamar had expected something almost evil, or at least seductive, some aura of people being lured into decadence, but it wasn't like that at all. It seemed contrived, almost silly.

They had no trouble getting into any of the bars, buying drinks, even catching glimpses of some very odd shows. In one of them, there was something done to a cigarette that Tamar preferred to wipe from her mind. It wasn't frightening, though, not in the least. The whole neighborhood seemed like a very low-budget stage show.

They didn't stay long in one place. They made the rounds, sometimes just looking through the doorway for a minute. To Tamar it was a blur of colored lights and alcohol and sweat and makeup. She was disappointed that it wasn't more exciting, but glad to have seen for herself. When it was time to leave, she thought, now I've seen it, and I have no reason ever to come back.

By the time they got back to Ciara's house, though, they were exhausted. Tamar fell asleep instantly. Right after an early breakfast with Ciara's host family she hopped on the bus. She was sure she would be in trouble, and she wanted to get it overwith.

When she got off the bus, though, and walked down the *soi*, along the glass-topped wall, and through the wrought-iron gate, she felt an inner warmth. She started to smile, and then she suddenly realized what she was feeling. It was familiarity, attachment. She was glad to be home.

She wallowed in the feeling as she climbed up the stairs, kicked off her shoes, and opened the door. She wiped the sweat off her face with her handkerchief, looked at a couple of *jinjuks* running up the wall and thought, six months here, and it feels like home. She was feeling so good about it that she got out a pen and paper and practiced the Thai alphabet.

No one seemed mad at her, either. She guessed maybe they were all out most of the night, or they forgot what day she was coming home. It didn't matter, and she didn't ask.

Chapter 14

In October, Tamar's father brought his new wife on a round-the-world trip, and they stopped in Bangkok for a visit. She went to have lunch with them at their hotel, the Imperial, the fancy one, right by the river. Tamar could have taken a taxi, but it seemed such a waste of money. She chose to take the bus.

She passed through the gate in front of her house and went into the street. She walked more carefully than usual, but the dirt still found its way inside her shoes and onto her clothes. Her hair was pinned up away from her face, as if she were on her way to school, but her outfit made her feel like a tourist. Why had she chosen to dress like such a *farang*, her short-sleeved shirt tucked into her pink pants? She felt more self-conscious than usual.

At the bus stop, two girls giggled behind the white collars of their school uniforms. An old woman in a sarong held two mesh bags full of groceries. The roar from an approaching bus was even louder than the clamor of the *tanon*. Tamar looked up and saw that it was the #93. She put out her hand to call it over.

When it had slowed enough, she leapt on and began pushing her way through the crowd in the aisle to the middle of the bus, where there was usually a bit more space, at least room to breathe. She found a spot where she could hold on to the bar along the ceiling and actually feel a bit of the moving air as it came through the open windows. Back home, she could barely reach the bars on the roofs of buses and subway trains, but here she was tall, and the bars were low enough for her to reach with bent elbows.

She heard the bus conductor clicking his way toward her. When he approached her, she expertly reached into her pocket with her left hand, keeping her right hand securely on the bar, and brought out two baht. As the bus swerved violently, she handed the money to the conductor, and he gave her a ticket. For a moment, she felt like an expert, very Thai. Then she thought about what she looked like, and became self-conscious again.

The smells of Bangkok came through the windows, the price for the breeze created by the speed of the bus. Rotting fruit mingled with sinus-clearing spices, under a pervasive layer of sweat. She was more used to it now, though. It really didn't seem that bad. She watched as a woman in a seat offered to hold the schoolbooks of the girl standing in the aisle next to her. Tamar had been very surprised the first time she observed this custom. She generally considered Thai bus manners quite rude. It was rare for anyone to give up a seat, even for an old person or a pregnant woman, and everyone was pressed so tightly against everyone else in the aisles that it was easy for the men to grope at the women, which they frequently did. She had gotten pretty good at dodging them. They did do this one thing, though, hold strangers' bags. She tried to imagine that happening in L.A. or New York. It was impossible. She never once saw anyone try to steal anything, either. They seemed to be very honorable about it. She thought she would never understand Thai culture.

After about an hour on the #93, she got off at Siam Square, where the movie theaters and Dunkin' Donuts and McDonald's were, and transferred to the air-conditioned #2. Air-conditioned buses cost five baht, but she thought it would be worth it. She found a seat by the window, and watched the banks and hotels and embassies on *Tanon Silom* go by.

She hadn't seen so many *farang* since the International School. They all seemed to be shopping, almost all of them dressed in shorts and skimpy tops. She knew that in the eyes of the Thais, they might as well be walking around town in nothing but g-strings and glitter. She knew they didn't mean any harm, but she was embarrassed to be thought one of them. On the other hand, she knew that all the prices in this area were inflated 500 to 1000 per cent, sometimes more, so the Thais at least made a profit on the situation. Even at those prices, things still seemed cheap to the average *farang* tourist, so maybe it was a symbiotic relationship. Maybe nobody really minded. Still, the whole arrangement made her uneasy. She didn't like thinking about it.

She took the #2 to the end of the line, almost to the river, and just a few blocks from the Imperial Hotel. She felt the heat when she first stepped into it again, but as she walked she became as oblivious to it as usual.

She was assailed by hawkers yelling "Lay-DEE! Lay-DEE! You lahk? Velly nahss!" and showing her cheap trinkets. She saw some men offering to help tourist ladies with their luggage, ushering them into taxis. They called the women "Madam", or at least that was what it sounded like at first. There seemed to be something odd about their pronunciation. It didn't sound like an ordinary Thai accent. Then she listened closely to the tones. They weren't saying "Madam". They were saying "*mah dum*", black dog. Tamar thought that was a brilliant piece of nastiness. Here they were calling these women names, and the women were giving them tips, probably big ones. She wondered if there were other phrases like that. There might be a whole vocabulary of disguised epithets.

A large, white building rose in front of her. It was the Imperial. She crossed the semi-circular driveway, between limousines, and walked up a wide set of white steps to the gold-trimmed glass door. A doorman in full livery opened it for her, smiled, and said, "Good morning." She returned his greeting, thinking how unbearably hot he must be in his uniform.

As she passed through the doorway, the air-conditioning hit her, shocking her body into goosebumps and shivers. It was much stronger than the air-conditioning on the bus. She looked around at the cool cleanliness of the lobby, and realized how sweaty and dirty she must be. She looked for a place to clean up.

She saw a restroom sign across the huge expanse of the lobby, on the other side of an artificial waterfall. As she crossed the room she passed people dressed in Western clothes, and others in various national costumes. She heard French, German, and some Middle Eastern language, Japanese and something African, as well as English. No Thai.

She was glad the bathroom was empty. It was spotless, and decorated in gilt and marble. Golden faucets led clear water into marble sinks. Golden paper towel holders suspended thick, soft, white paper towels over marble counters. The toilets were all Western style.

Tamar washed at least the surface dirt from her face and hands and tried to comb her hair with her fingers. She still looked filthy in these spotless surroundings, but at least she was more comfortable. Her body had adjusted to the temperature enough to stop shivering.

She walked back into the lobby and over to the hotel telephones and called room 305. Ted Kelly answered the phone.

"Hello."

"Dad?"

"Hey there! Are you here?"

"Yeah, in the lobby."

"Great! Come on up. It's 305."

"I know. I'll be right there."

There was a man in the elevator to push the button for her. The doors opened smoothly and soundlessly on the third floor. It was cool and quiet in the hallway. 305 wasn't very far. She knocked on the door.

He opened it and there he was, a big man, with red hair that matched Tamar's, and clear blue eyes. He smiled, that bright, charming, always optimistic smile, and hugged her. He told her it was great to see her, she looked fantastic, and Karen would be out in a minute so why didn't she just have a seat.

The room had two levels. Stairs led up from the living room area to a loft that contained the bedroom and bathroom. The walls and furniture were decorated with expensive-looking fabrics in shades of blue and white, and there were Belgian chocolates and a large basket of tropical fruit on the coffee table.

The sound of a blow dryer ceased, and a few minutes later Karen came down the stairs. She was tall and lean, with straight, brown hair and high cheekbones. She was only about ten years older than Tamar, but she looked very serious, very business-like.

She gripped Tamar's hand firmly and looked her in the eye as she said hello. Tamar tried to remember what she did for a living. It was something political, campaign managing or something. She was probably good at it.

She looked at them as they sat together on the couch. They looked happy. They looked like a couple. They always did, in the beginning. She looked in her father's eyes. Everybody said they sparkled, or twinkled, or glinted. They said he showed his Irish heritage, that he was the life of the party, had the gift of the gab.

It was all true, but she saw something else there. She saw sadness, pain, sometimes even desperation. Sometimes she thought she was making it up, because no one else seemed to see it, but then she remembered things like when he split up with Sandra, his third wife, and he called her all the time. She had been only twelve years old, but he would call late at night, when she should have been asleep. He would just ask her how her day had been, and what she was doing the next day, but the sound in his voice, like he was on the verge not just of crying but of bursting into pieces, like glass too long in the freezer, was frightening to her. She pretended not to hear it. She never asked him how he was. She just kept her voice bright and happy and got off the phone as quickly as she could.

She wished she could just not worry about his pain. Sometimes she tried to think of him as a distant relative, or a character in a story, or someone else she could feel sad for without feeling so trapped by the feeling, but it never worked. Instead, she felt like he was a heavy boulder sinking to the bottom of the ocean, and she was tied to him and couldn't get free.

Since she couldn't seem not to care, she tried not to think about caring. She tried to push all that aside, somewhere she couldn't see it, but then he would do something like show up in Bangkok, where she thought she would be far enough away, with his new wife, and his optimistic smile, and she just knew it wouldn't work. In a few years it would be the same again. He'd be sinking again, and she'd be fighting the weight of him.

"So, are you ready to eat?" he said.

"Absolutely!" She smiled as brightly as he did.

They went downstairs to lunch. They had fresh, beautifully presented salads, just as they would have had in New York or L.A. Tamar looked at her father as he was telling her something about how business was going. She nodded. She said, "Really?" and "Great!" She ate her salad.

"So, Tamar, what do you think we should see while we are here?" Karen asked.

"Definitely the Grand Palace, if you haven't seen it already, and you should go up to Ayuttaya and see the ruins, if you have time. People say the floating market is great, but I haven't been there."

"The heat is amazing. Do you ever get used to it?"

"I think I have, pretty much, but I'm very grateful to whoever invented the handkerchief."

"I'm sure. You know, it is amazing how much you two look alike. Except for the color of the eyes, you have the same face."

She had heard that since she was very small, that she looked so much like him, that she was so much like him. He seemed to like to think they were kindred spirits, and she let him. When she saw him, she talked about the things he liked to talk about, listened to the things he wanted to say. She supposed when she was younger she did it for his attention. Maybe that was still the reason, but she thought that now she did it more because it was what he expected, something he relied on. She didn't think it was for his attention anymore, because now she realized his attention wasn't really on her, it was on the idea he had of her, the idea that here was a person like him, who understood him, who loved him, who would always be in his life. She felt that he needed her, and she hated him for it.

Perhaps she didn't really hate him. Maybe it was something else. After all, she must love him, or she wouldn't care so much. Maybe it was the other way around. Maybe what she hated was that she needed him, that she wanted him to love her so badly, the real her, not his idea of what he wanted her to be, but the real Tamar, who wasn't like him, not really, or at least didn't want to be.

It was that that she hated, that she needed something from him that he would probably never be able to give, but that, despite that, she kept trying to give him what he needed from her. She pretended to be what he wanted her to be, she told him the things she knew he wanted to hear, even though she knew it was no use, that he would never really look at her, that as charming as he was, as good as he was at making people feel at ease, and making people like him and admire him, his gaze would never truly leave the confines of his own unquenchable need. His camouflaged desperation was a wall he would never see her through, and she knew it, but she couldn't stop trying. She couldn't stop caring. She wanted more than anything not to care.

When lunch was over, Tamar walked back through the lobby, out of the air-conditioning, and into the street. She passed through the hawkers and the tourists to the bus stop. She decided not to bother with air-conditioning. When the #77 slowed down, she hopped on. It was unusually uncrowded. There was one completely empty seat, and she took it. She looked out the window, letting the Bangkok air, with its stench and its grit, assault her face.

She got off at Siam Square, to wait for the #93. There was no one else waiting at the stop. She listened to the traffic as she untucked her shirt, and let its tails hang far down over her pink pants.

She kept the tears back all the way along *Tanon Chulalongkorn*, all the way down the *soi*, and all the way up the stairs, but there was no one in the bedroom but the *jinjuks* and the spiders, so she climbed up to the loft, put her face in her pillow, and lay there crying until dinner.

Chapter 15

By November, the rain was less predictable. It no longer came every day. There was a festival at this time of year called *Loy Kratong*, in which people floated candles down the river, a sort of festival of lights. Noelle's host family was having a party, and all the students in Bangkok were invited. Some people were even coming in from out of town.

When Tamar arrived, there were already more than a hundred people there, being loud, drinking and eating. Most of the FSA students were gathered around a table in a pavilion near the river, already dotted with floating candles. Noelle handed her a drink immediately. It was fruity, mango, pineapple, probably other things too. She had another one immediately after.

Everybody was in a party mood, looking forward to being drunk and wild. At first Tamar was concerned about Noelle's host family, but all the guests seemed to be letting go fairly thoroughly, and no one was paying any attention to the foreign students. She'd had alcohol before, but she didn't like the taste of it, and she'd never really been drunk. She thought, why not give it a try. Everyone seems to think it's such fun, and these taste good. She had a third drink.

By the fourth drink, she was starting to feel sick, not just sick to her stomach, but sick as if she had the flu. Her head felt heavy and her thinking was sluggish. She had to concentrate to understand what people were saying. She felt like she had some terrible virus, and she was afraid she was going to throw up. She thought, so this is what being drunk is like. It doesn't seem like much fun, but maybe it gets better.

She didn't see Ciara, but she did see Ben. He suddenly appeared beside her.

"Are you okay?" he asked.

"Maybe not."

"Why don't you sit down."

"Okay."

He brought her some food. At first she didn't want it, but when she started eating she felt a little better.

"I never really had much to drink before," she said.

"Me neither."

"It doesn't really seem like that much fun."

"It doesn't look like that much fun."

"They seem like they're having a good time."

Joel, Noelle and Nerissa were dancing around each other with their drinks in their hands, laughing as they nearly fell.

"Maybe," said Ben, "or maybe they're just pretending."

"Could be. People pretend a lot of things."

He looked at her with an expression of confusion, or maybe concern.

"I read The Great Gatsby," he said. "You were right. People at school said they didn't like it, but it was good."

"I'm glad you liked it. I think it's hard for people to like things if they have to read them in school."

"It's hard to like something you're forced to do."

"Exactly."

"Are you feeling any better?"

"Yeah. The food definitely helps. Thanks."

"Sure."

"So, Ben, tell me more about Nebraska."

"Why do you want to hear about Nebraska? It's boring."

"No it's not. It's nice."

"Nice! I think that's worse than boring."

Ciara walked up, full of enthusiasm, and said, "How's the party going?"

Tamar looked around. "It seems to be going pretty well," she said.

"Do you need a drink?"

"No, thanks. I just stopped feeling sick."

"Then let's dance."

"I don't know if that's a good idea."

"Come on. You'll be fine."

"Okay."

"Ben, are you coming?" Ciara asked.

"That's all right," he said. "I'll stay here."

They joined Joel's group, which had grown larger, and danced for most of the night. Tamar didn't drink anymore, and she didn't feel sick anymore. A few other people threw up in the bushes, and she was glad she wasn't one of them. She was glad Ben had gotten her to eat when he did.

She waved to him a few times while she was dancing. When the party was over she looked for him, to thank him again, but he had already left. She took a taxi home, and she barely managed to stay awake long enough to get upstairs and into bed.

She woke up the next morning tired and thirsty, but feeling surprisingly good. She thought, overall, it had been a pretty good party.

Chapter 16

Tamar grew to enjoy her routine, her classes at school, her proficiency in Thai, her ability to judge how high to hold her *wai*, but she was excited for the next trip. It was to the northeast, for some sort of elephant festival, and some other tourist sites.

On the ride up they got near the Cambodian border. There was apparently some skirmishing, and they had to take a detour. They were ordered to turn by soldiers with guns. They could hear distant explosions and see smoke. It was like the attempted coup, though, in that nothing really happened to them, and it didn't quite seem real. Tamar didn't feel in danger at all. She was just excited to be able to say she saw soldiers and smoke.

The place they stayed was a group of huts like the place at Pang Nga, only this was in a sort of swampy jungle, and the mosquitoes were like locusts. There was netting on the beds, but some could get through. Tamar tried to sleep with her hands over her face. She was covered in bites.

The elephants were entertaining, though. They were used as taxis in town, at least during this festival. Riding an elephant was like riding a giant horse in slow motion. Their walking gait felt just like a canter, but very slow.

There were shows in which elephants pushed heavy things and stepped over people. There was a recreation of some ancient battle, but Tamar didn't really understand it. It just looked like a lot of elephants running around an arena. That in itself was impressive, though, and loud.

After the elephants, they went to the Bridge on the River Kwai site. PiLahng explained that it wasn't the real Bridge on the River Kwai. It was a location they used for the movie. They had fireworks there at night. Tamar thought, I come to the other side of the world to see something different, and I get an outpost of the Universal Studios tour.

The next day, though, they drove up to a mountain and went to a famous waterfall, pool after pool of clear water you could swim in. The boys could wear their bathing suits and no shirts, but the girls had to wear bulky T-shirts and long shorts.

It made it hard to swim, but the water was cool and soothing. Tamar wanted to stay all day. They were all calm and quiet on the bus after that. When her hair dried, Tamar was shocked by how soft it was.

Duncan said he'd been to see Selena. He said she seemed okay, but she was on medication, and they wouldn't let her leave the hospital yet. They didn't think it was safe to put her on a plane back to Australia. That's all he would say about it.

One day, they were on the bus, and Tamar was curled up on a seat by herself, napping. Ben and Duncan were a couple of seats away. She woke up at the sound of her name. It took her a few moments to be conscious enough to follow the conversation. She didn't open her eyes. Ben said, "I don't know what it is. She's not really beautiful, like in a magazine or something, but there's something about her."

Duncan said, "She's lovely."

"Yes. She's lovely."

They were quiet for a while after that, and Tamar fell asleep again, but later, she kept thinking about that bit of conversation. She wasn't sure she had really heard it, or that, if she had, it had been about her, but she thought so.

It gave her a gentle, warm feeling to think about it, more than just being flattered. She had thought Ben might be interested in her, but, unlike many of the other girls, she wasn't looking for a boyfriend. She liked learning Thai and adjusting to the culture and doing things on her own. She liked the sense of independence and freedom it gave her. She didn't want to have someone expecting her to want to see him all the time, to look longingly in his eyes, to be in love.

Maybe he didn't want that though. There wasn't any point in wasting time worrying about it. She spent most of her time with Ciara, but she did find herself watching Ben sometimes, to see if he was watching her. She started to think she might not mind if he was.

Chapter 17

PiLahng wanted the students in Bangkok to present a sort of traveling Christmas show to all their schools. Ben's house was more or less centrally located, and he had somehow gotten hold of a Santa suit, so they met there. The house was very far down a winding *soi*. It was possible to walk from the *tanon*, but he had said it took about half an hour, and Tamar was running late. *Dtukdtuks* didn't generally hang around such out of the way places, and if they did, the ride would be expensive. For a few baht, the motorcycle guys would take you down the *soi*.

Tamar was nervous. Motorcycles were dangerous enough under any circumstances, but she would have to ride sidesaddle on the back, with no helmet or protective clothing whatsoever, and she would have to be very careful not only to stay on, but also not to touch the driver, because all the drivers were male.

She had never been on a motorcycle, but she had ridden horses, and she had the idea of thinking of a motorcycle as a horse. A horse and rider work together, adjusting to each other's movements. When she was on a horse, she didn't worry about falling off, even though she could, because she felt attached. She felt as though she and the horse were one being. She knew the motorcycle was just a machine, and couldn't adjust to her movements, but she was so scared she had to try something. She climbed on, balanced, and held on tight, and then she closed her eyes and pretended she was on a horse. She was surprised to find that her tactic worked. She felt attached to the motorcycle, even though she was perched gingerly on the back, holding on with one hand, and she never slipped.

Ben's house was small, but clean and well-organized. Tamar was the last one to arrive, and they had already started without her. They were singing "Silent Night" when she walked in the door.

Ben seemed to enjoy playing the host. He didn't pay Tamar any particular attention, just saw to everyone's needs. She sat next to Ciara, who had a beautiful voice, and practiced songs with everyone else. She did catch Ben staring at her once, while he was refilling glasses, but only briefly.

That was the only rehearsal they had. PiLahng had a friend who had lent her a *bokbok*, and they drove around to all the schools in Bangkok to sing carols Christmas week, instead of going to school. They were a big hit everywhere they went, especially Ben. In the Santa suit, he wasn't his usual quiet self. He clowned around and made all the kids laugh.

The next Monday, Tamar headed down the stairs and over to the kitchen for breakfast. As she reached the bottom of the stairs, she was suddenly hit with a feeling of being at her grandparents' house in Florida. She tried to pinpoint what made her feel that way. She finally decided it was that the air felt different, and it smelled different. It smelled just like Grandma and Grandpa's backyard.

The thought almost made her cry. Her grandparents' house was her favorite place in the world. Grandma and Grandpa Silver were her favorite people. She was always happy to have a reason to visit them.

They lived on a quiet lake in Florida. Her grandfather had been a navy man, and he had a small boat they took out on the lake, and a larger one they took fishing in the Gulf of Mexico. They had been athletes in their youth, she a gymnast, he a track star, and they were still very active, more full of energy than anyone else she knew, of any age. They swam and rowed and golfed and fished and hiked and traveled and she loved to do it all with them.

They had been married more than forty years, and they were still obviously in love. She could tell by the way they called each other Joey and Evie, by the way they looked each other, by the warmth between them even when they fought.
Her favorite thing, though, was to watch him give her presents. He never gave her just one present. It was always at least two or three, and they were always romantic presents, perfume, jewelry, peignoirs. Sometimes he gave her something more practical, but only if he knew it was something she wanted and wouldn't buy

for herself. He didn't give her just any romantic present either. If it was perfume it was her favorite scent. If it was a peignoir it was exactly her size and in one of her favorite colors. If it was jewelry, it was perfectly her style, nothing garish or too big, something attention-getting but elegant.

Tamar loved the whole process of his giving her a present. Grandma always seemed so happy, so genuinely delighted that he would think to get her something, even though he always did, for every important occasion, and sometimes for no reason at all. She would open it with a big smile on her face, and it would get even bigger when she saw what it was. It was always something that showed not just how much he loved her, but how well he knew her, and it made Tamar's heart swell to see it.

The best moment of all, though, was the look on his face when he saw the look on hers. The joy he felt in making her so happy filled not just his smile and his eyes but the whole house. She had never in her life felt a house so full of love.

Grandma took good care of the house too. She seemed to have a magical ability to make it welcoming and cheerful. It was always spotless, everything always neatly in its place, and yet she never seemed to clean it, or at least Tamar rarely saw her cleaning anything. It was as if the dust disappeared of its own accord. It wasn't like so many clean houses, either, sterile, so that you were afraid to touch anything in it. Everyone felt free and relaxed in Grandma's house. It was the best place in the world.

Tamar had long ago stopped trying to describe her grandparents and their house to people. Everyone always thought she was exaggerating, or even making it up, but she wasn't. They really did have some kind of magic, something she had never seen or felt anywhere else, and here, today, she felt like she was there.

Later as she walked down the *soi*, she kept trying to pinpoint what it was that made the air like it was on the lake in Florida. Perhaps a new flower had bloomed, or a storm was coming.

She had been waiting at the bus stop for a few minutes when she was struck by the realization that she had not used her handkerchief once that morning. She felt her face. Not one bead of sweat. It was late December. It must be the cold season! It was supposed to last well into February. Could there really be a couple of months of no sweating and everything smelling like Grandma and Grandpa's house?

She was full of energy all day. She nearly forgot to be disrespectful to the computer teacher.

By the next Monday, she needed her handkerchief again. It didn't get anywhere near the heat of April, but the real, handkerchief-free cold season only lasted a week. It was a good week, though.

Chapter 18

In January, Ciara invited Tamar to join a group of FSA students who were taking a trip up to Chiang Mai. Rowena and the party girls weren't going, and Tamar very much wanted to go up north. It was the one region of the country she hadn't seen yet, and they were taking the train. She loved trains.

They met at the station. The group was Ciara, Justine, Noelle, Fransje, Tamar and the three Norwegian boys. They watched as the terrain changed from industrial Bangkok to rice paddies, to drier farmland, to forest, to mountain valleys. Tamar was fascinated by the shapes of the mountains. She had seen the soft slopes of the Appalachians, and the solid peaks of the Rockies, but these were entirely different, not remotely cone-shaped. They had a grace, an airiness. They looked exactly like the mountains in Chinese wall hangings, rounded cliffs, seemingly created with one stroke of the brush. Tamar had always thought those paintings were stylized, an accepted representation of a mountain, more elegant than the real thing, but now she saw that was not the case at all. Eventually the green mountain valleys gave way to cityscape again.

Chiang Mai was a smaller, cleaner, cooler version of Bangkok. It had the same little stall shops, and the same tourist area with neon signs in English. They had reservations at a small guesthouse on a busy street. They bought *gutio* for dinner, and then they all crammed into one room to sleep, some on the beds, some on the floor.

The next day they met their guide Sombat, tall for a Thai, with long hair. He didn't smile much, or talk more than necessary. The general impression he gave was one of serenity, which gave Tamar an instinctive confidence in his abilities.

They were joined by two blond Austrian couples, who didn't speak much English, or perhaps preferred not to. The twelve of them climbed into a pickup truck and headed to the edge of town. They didn't know exactly where they'd be going, just that they would be trekking through the mountains, and would sleep each night in a different village, and that all their meals would be provided.

The first day seemed to be straight uphill the whole time. They walked on a narrow dirt road through thick woods. It was pretty, and quiet, but both monotonous and strenuous. There was almost no conversation. Everyone was too tired.

Around mid-afternoon, they came to the top of a rise. Across a small valley, on another slope, they could see a small cluster of huts in a large clearing. Sombat said, "First village. Lisu village."

By the time they actually reached the village, the sun was starting to set. A couple of small children in school uniforms ran up to them, followed by some of their more sedate elders. The children *wai*-ed to them all and spoke to Sombat. They acted as translators, because the adults didn't speak Thai. They were Lisu, and they had their own language, and their own unofficial province up in the hills.

The group was directed to a large hut. It seemed like a school. It had a rollaway chalkboard at one end, and benches in rows. At the back was a large platform with a pile of blankets on it that would serve as their bed.

They put down their backpacks and were attempting to catch their breath when they heard a strange sound, like a cow with a sore throat. Tamar was curious and went outside. As she looked around, the sound became a kind of shriek. Some of the others came outside too. Then she saw it. At the other end of the village, a group of people around a huge, black pig.

"Are they killing it?" asked Fransje.

"I think that's our dinner." Said Ciara.

"I'll go hungry," said Justine, the vegetarian.

"Are they cooking it with that?" asked Fransje.

One of the villagers had lit what looked like a torch and was scorching the pig with it.

"Maybe they're burning off the bristles." Tamar suggested.

"I can't stand this." Justine went back inside.

Several of the people took out enormous knives and started scraping the pig with them.

"Are they scraping off the bristles or the skin?" asked Ciara.

"I think I've seen enough now," said Tamar. "I'll eat whatever they serve us though. I'm starving."

"I'll eat my own hand soon." Said Fransje. "That lunch was very small."

Whatever the dinner was, it was delicious. Only Justine refused the meat and had plain rice. They ate around a huge campfire. It seemed that the whole village was there in one big circle.

When she was full, Tamar was suddenly exhausted, and left the campfire for the hut. It was very dark as she walked down the one dirt road through town, but she didn't realize how dark until she got past a couple of huts along the way and was suddenly out of sight of the campfire. She felt like a cartoon character suddenly realizing he's run off a cliff. She couldn't see anything, not even the ground under her feet. She thought, if there were a cliff two feet in front of me, I would walk right off it. She couldn't see a hut, a tree, anything. She thought of the old cliché and put her hand in front of her face. It was true. She really couldn't see it. She spread her hands out in front of her and shuffled. She was afraid to lift her feet up for fear of where she might put them down. She knew it was completely irrational, but she had an idea that if she took a foot off the ground it might fall away, just disappear, and she would put her foot down again into a bottomless pit.

Her right hand touched something. It felt like the wall of a hut. She tried to remember the layout of the village, and thought that this was the hut next to the big one, so she felt along the wall to the end, shuffling all the way, and prepared to let go and try to find the big hut. Before she did, she took a few deep breaths. The air was chilly, but fresh. During one of these breaths, she looked up, and almost fell over.

There were stars, an uncountable number of stars. The sky looked white, with little black dots. She looked down toward the ground again, because she couldn't believe that the sky was that bright and the land was that dark, but it was. She didn't see the moon, but how could you find it in all that white, and the thing that was really shocking, the thing that made her nearly fall over, was that it seemed so close. It seemed like it might fall on her any minute, or that if she jumped as high as she could she could almost touch it.

She thought, so this is night without lights, this was night for the cavemen. No wonder ancient people studied the stars. They're all that exist at night. There is nothing here but stars and blackness, and whatever might be out there that I can't see. She felt nervous and disoriented, but thrilled by the intensity of the sky, so she took one more breath, let go of the hut, stuck her hands out again, and shuffled forward, looking up all the way.

Finally her right hand brushed against something, just slightly. It was the corner of a hut. She had nearly missed it. She worked her way around the corner, and then she could see light coming out of the doorway. She felt rescued, as if she had been shipwrecked. She came through the door, ready to tell her emotional tale, and found no one there to tell, just a candle burning by the chalkboard, and the Austrians already asleep on the platform. She remembered how tired she was, took a blanket off the pile, and curled up to sleep.

The next day was a bit less steep, but still very much uphill. The forest was less dense, though, and so they could catch mountain views between the trees. The road became a path, and in some areas they had to walk single file.

When they were almost to the top of a particular rise, Sombat made them stop. He told them they were about to walk through a small valley, and that they should stick to the path, stay in single file, and be quiet. He said it could be dangerous if they didn't. He looked so absolutely serious that they followed his instructions.

They filed over the ridge and into the valley. It was small, maybe as long as a football field, with a narrow path right down the middle and steep slopes up each side. Both slopes were absolutely covered in beautiful red and white flowers. Tamar wondered what could be so dangerous about that until she noticed that atop each ridge were concrete bunkers, and sticking out of the bunkers were what could very likely be the barrels of powerful guns. It took her a minute, but then she understood that the flowers were poppies, and that they were walking right through an outpost of the heroin trade. She kept her hands very close to her sides after that. She wanted to make sure they knew she wasn't touching any of their poppies. She couldn't believe they'd let tourists walk right through their field. She guessed there must be some sort of arrangement involved, but she preferred not to think about it too much.

That night's village was Meo. It was similar to the Lisu village, but hidden among the trees, instead of in a clearing, and on a very steep slope. Tamar was a bit worried about wandering around at night, but it turned out they didn't have to. There was a very large hut which seemed to be a sort of meeting room, and that was where they ate and slept.

After dinner their hosts asked them to sit with them in a large circle. Tamar thought they were being asked to participate in some sort of hospitality ritual, especially when one of them brought out a two foot long piece of bamboo, with a little piece of bamboo sticking out near the bottom. It wasn't until he lit it that she realized it was a homemade bong. It was passed around the circle. It seemed rude to refuse, but Tamar didn't breathe in very hard. She wasn't sure what was in it. She slipped out of the circle before it came around again. On her way to the sleeping area she passed by a group of elderly villagers, lying on their sides and smoking pipes. Their eyes were very red, and the smoke around them smelled like burned molasses. She guessed that must be opium. It was a very strong smell, but it wasn't so noticeable where she would sleep. She went as far from them as she could, on the other side of a pile of blankets.

The third day was much less uphill. In fact there was a great deal of downhill. It was much easier, but Justine wasn't feeling well. She'd been eating nothing but plain rice, and not much of that. She said it wasn't that, that she had some kind of flu. Whatever it was, the trek was becoming very difficult for her. Noelle said she wasn't feeling well either. When they reached the Karen village that evening, Justine and Noelle were shipped back to Chiang Mai in a pickup truck. Tamar wasn't sure how, since she didn't see anything one could call a road, but she felt sure they would be fine.

Once the truck was out of hearing range, the Karen village was very peaceful. They could hear the river, not far away. Tamar was excited about the next day. The hiking was just about over.

Tomorrow they would be on the water. They would be rafting back to Chiang Mai.

Chapter 19

It was a little bit warmer, at this lower elevation, and Tamar slept very comfortably. She woke up early, ready for rafting. It took less than an hour to walk down the path to the river. They were surrounded by tall, straight, green bamboo trees all the way down. As they neared the water, they saw some of the villagers chopping down some of the trees. By the edge, a couple of the men had several bamboo trunks in a row on the ground, and they were tying them together. At one end they attached a crude tripod, made of thinner bamboo stalks.

"Oh my God." Tamar said to Fransje. "That's our raft."

"Not a very strong looking raft."

"I don't know why I had this image in my mind of a big yellow raft and lifejackets for everyone. I guess that was pretty stupid."

"No. I had the same idea."

Ciara came up from behind them. "Is that our raft?"

"We think so."

They made three rafts, and there was a villager to pilot each one. The only steering instrument was another long bamboo stalk to use as a pole. Tamar, Ciara and Fransje shared a raft with Sombat and a villager named Tao. The boys were on the second raft, and the Austrians on the third. The rafts sat just under the surface of the water, rather than on top. That was why the tripods were needed to keep their bags dry.

They started down the river, all more or less together. It was smooth at first, but the water was cold, and they were sitting right in it.

They went around a bend, and the river widened. There were large rocks they had to maneuver around, and the current seemed to be moving faster. There was some whitewater, near the rocks. The boys' raft made too wide a turn around a rock and got stuck on the bank. They were still struggling to push off as Tamar's raft went around the next bend and lost sight of them. The water got rougher. Soon it could really be called rapids. The raft bounced and swayed. Tamar looked at the cords that held it together and hoped they were strong.

They made a wide turn to the right of a rock, and the Austrians' raft passed them on the left and rushed around another bend. When they came around the same bend, a little closer to the middle of the river, they saw the other raft in pieces, stuck among the branches of a large tree that hung into the water. The Austrians and their raft guide were all on the bank, looking wet and scratched, but they responded to shouts of "Are you OK?" with nods.

The girls' raft continued over the rapids. There were trees all along the edges here, so they had to stay in the middle, but there were big rocks there. As they turned a little too quickly around one, the raft tilted far sideways, and Tamar slid into the water. She had just enough time during the fall to notice a large rock directly ahead. She opened her eyes, but all she could see was white, churning water. She didn't know which way to swim. All she knew was she was moving fast, and that rock was close. She flailed around, looking for sky.

Part of her was very frightened, imagining her impending impact with the big rock, but another part of her seemed to be watching calmly, wondering why she couldn't see anything, which way the rock was, which way was up, which way down. The calm part realized her aimless struggling was useless. She didn't know whether she was making things better or worse. She thought, either I will hit the rock or I won't, but I don't seem to have much control over the situation. She tried to think of anything she could do that might actually be helpful. It occurred to her that she could try to protect her head. She reached her arms up to fold them around it.

Something grabbed her arm and yanked her in some direction. Her head came out of the water and she saw that Ciara was pulling her by the wrist. Ciara's eyes and mouth went wide. She pulled Tamar back on the raft just as they passed the rock. Another few seconds and she would have hit it. Once she was solidly on the raft again, wet and shivering, Ciara started laughing.

"What's so funny?" Tamar asked.

"I don't know. I guess I'm nervous or something. I have never seen anyone look so terrified!"

"I was! I thought I was going to hit that big rock. Thanks for pulling me up."

"You looked so strange waving your hands around under the water."

"I don't care. I'm just glad you grabbed me."

Tamar was surprised that she didn't seem to have swallowed any water. She must have been holding her breath the whole time. She hadn't thought about breathing at all. She supposed that if she had been underwater much longer it would have been all she could think about. The sight of that rock passing by her feet as she climbed onto the raft kept going through her mind. She had been close enough to see its rough surface. She knew if she had hit it she would be bleeding. She hadn't hit it, though. Ciara had been there to pull her up. The last remnants of her fear dissipated and were replaced by gratefulness, not just to Ciara, but in general. It was a very primitive feeling, grateful not to be bleeding, or seriously injured, or dead. She wondered if she really might have died.

The river became gradually calmer. Soon they could see a small dock with a hut next to it. The raft pulled right up to it, but it was about three feet from the surface of the water to the surface of the dock, so they had to climb up onto it.

Standing on the dock, Tamar suddenly had a rush of feeling. She felt like a caveman who had just killed a saber-toothed tiger. She felt as if she had climbed a high mountain. She felt like she could climb Mt. Everest, or do anything else. She didn't mind the water or the rock or the raft. She had been in danger, and she had beaten it, conquered it somehow. It made her feel invincible.

It seemed silly to her, to feel like a conquering hero just for taking a raft down a stretch of river that probably wasn't nearly as dangerous as it had seemed, but that didn't stop the feeling. She felt taller, stronger, braver.

The Austrians came walking along very soon, but it was late afternoon by the time the boys showed up. After they freed themselves from the bank, they had smashed up on some rocks and ended up on the opposite side of the river. They had to climb up a waterfall, and then walk downriver well past the dock, to a place where they could safely cross. They were completely exhausted.

The same orange Toyota pickup truck that had taken Justine and Noelle the day before was there to take them the rest of the way into Chiang Mai. As they jolted down the road, Tamar thought about the river, how powerful it was, and how unpredictable. She thought about how easy it was for those flimsy bamboo rafts to smash up on the rocks and trees, and how afraid she was when she fell off. She thought, if I did it again, would I fall off again? Would I hit the rock? Would I drown? The conquering feeling was fading now, but she remembered it clearly. She wondered if she would have to do something dangerous to feel it again.

She had so many thoughts, so many feelings, that they all jumbled up in her head. She was glad she didn't have to think clearly. She could just sit and watch the trees thin out and the buildings appear as they rode into the city.

Chapter 20

The next day, clean and rested, they all went shopping in Chiang Mai. Tamar saw no reason to save her money anymore, since they would be leaving soon, so she spent most of what she had on souvenirs and gifts for people at home. She bought clothes like the ones the hill tribes wore, a carved teak elephant, beautiful coasters for Grandma's coaster collection. By the end of the day she had four full shopping bags.

Everyone else was going to stay another couple of days, but she had promised to be home, so she left that night. She took the night train from Chiang Mai to Bangkok. Since she was low on money, she went third class.

Everyone in the car stared at her as she sat down on one of the wooden slatted benches that served as seats. She assumed it was because she was the only *farang* in the car. The train started. She was pleased that she would have a whole bench to herself. It wasn't as uncomfortable as it looked.

After a couple of hours, a man came down the aisle selling snacks. He had shrimp crackers and bottles of orange soda in a basket. In his other hand he had a cylindrical money changing machine like the ones the bus conductors carried. He was clicking it the way they did, and calling his prices out to the passengers.

When he came to Tamar's bench, he said, in heavily accented English, "For you, for kiss." She glared at him. He shook his basket toward her and said it again. "For you, for kiss." Some of the passengers chuckled and whispered. "*Mai ao!*" she sneered at the snack man. "I don't want anything." The car erupted in the same "Oho!" sound she had heard in swordfighting class. She didn't know if that was because she told him no or because she did it in Thai. She was too tired to think about it much, though. She closed her eyes and listened to the train, but she didn't sleep.

The train pulled into Bangkok just after 5a.m. The sky was still dark. As Tamar tumbled out of the third class car, weighed down by her four shopping bags and longing for her bed, a swarm of taxi drivers converged on her.

"TakSEE! LayDEE!" they yelled. "TakSEE! LayDEE!" over and over.

"*Mai ao.*" she said, exhausted. "*Mai ao taxi.* I don't want one."

Despite her protestations, they followed her, en masse, out of the brightly lit station and onto the dark streets of Bangkok.

After about a block, all patience abandoned her. Under a lamppost, she threw her bags on the ground, and started a tirade, in Thai.

She said, "You are all wrong! You don't want me in your taxi! You think I'm some rich tourist. I'm not at all. Do you want to know how much money I have? Do you know how much money I have? I have seven and a half baht. Seven and a half baht! Does anyone want to take me across town for seven and a half baht?"

The taxi drivers burst into hysterics. The trip she needed to take would cost at least 100 baht. Seven and a half baht! That was hilarious!

Tamar continued, "What I need is the #93 bus. Can anyone tell me where the nearest bus stop is?"

They showered her with solicitude. She didn't know whether it was out of appreciation for her performance, or general good humor, but they brought out maps, pointed in the appropriate direction, and did not follow her when she picked up her four shopping bags and left. She thanked them, and headed down the block.

Tamar could still hear the taxi drivers laughing as she turned onto a quieter, darker street, following their directions. It was even starting to seem amusing to her. Bangkok taxi drivers weren't nearly as terrible as their reputation, she thought.

Then she noticed a taxi moving very slowly down the street. It was the only car on the road. It wasn't moving any faster than she was. She hoped it wasn't following her.

The driver yelled to her, in English, sort of, "I take you, for free. For free, I take you."

"No thank you," she said. "*Kao rot*. I'll take the bus."

The driver pulled over and got out of his cab. He was small and his movements were quick. He caught up to her and stood too close. His presence gave her a very sleazy bad feeling, as he continued to insist on driving her home, "for free."

She mentally took back her charitable thought about Bangkok taxi drivers, and began looking for escape routes. It was very dark and the streets were empty. She was very tired, and she didn't know her way around this part of town. She figured that her best bet was to drop her bags, kick off her flip-flop shoes, and run as fast as she could back to the train station.

As she was choosing her moment, another cab pulled up alongside her. For a moment she thought her chance was gone. Then she heard what the new driver was saying. In Thai, he said, "I'll take you to the bus stop. No charge."

Tamar ran through the possibilities. These guys could be working together. It could be some kind of trap. They might be completely unconnected to each other, but both equally dangerous. This new one could be even worse than the first one.

For some reason, though, she trusted this second driver. It might have been because he spoke to her respectfully, in Thai. It might have been because he just offered to take her the few blocks to the bus stop, and not, outrageously, all the way home. He could have been a skillful predator, and the first driver just a clumsy, overzealous good samaritan. She knew all the possibilities. She also knew she was too tired to run very fast, that the first guy frightened her, and that she trusted this new one.

All of this happened in less than a second, and then she grabbed all four shopping bags and climbed into the second driver's cab.

She kept her hand near the door handle, just in case, and thought, Oh God, please let this have been the right decision.

The driver asked her the usual questions: How long had she been in Bangkok? How did she like Thai food? Thai dancing? Thai people? She gave all the politic answers. He asked if she was married, engaged, had a boyfriend. She tried not to get too suspicious.

He started listing differences he had noticed between Americans and Thais, and talking about how much he liked American girls, and Tamar started to think this trip was getting to be longer than she had expected.

He turned into a very dark, narrow street, and she began to call herself unpleasant names in her mind. She should have run. Now she had no idea where she was.

He kept talking, although she was no longer listening, and weaving through tiny little dark streets. She tried to stay calm and to evaluate the weaponry capabilities of the things in her bags. She decided the souvenir wooden elephant had long, sharp tusks that might do. It was near the top of one of the bags. She tried surreptitiously to get to it with her left hand.

He made another turn, and suddenly there was light everywhere, bright streetlamps, cars with their lights on, flashlights held by people in uniforms, and buses, huge lines of buses, revved up, lit up, and ready to start their routes. He wasn't taking her to the bus stop. He had taken her to the bus depot. He pulled up right behind a #93. She couldn't believe it. The adrenaline was still rushing through her body, but she managed to gather together enough presence of mind to open the door and get out, and then to say thank you as she pulled out the four shopping bags. "*Kopkun mahk-ka*," she said. "*Kopkun mahkmahk-ka.*"

As she was pulling out the last bag, and just as her heartbeat was returning to normal, he grabbed her arm. She was baffled by this. Why now? Why after all this, when she was out of the cab.

He pulled down on her arm, and she looked at him, bewildered. "*Kao rot*," he said, and pointed to the bus. "*Kao rot.*" She didn't understand. Of course she was going to take the bus. That's what this was all about. "*Ka*," she said, "*kao rot.*"

He let go of her, and drove off. She didn't understand at all, but she was greatly relieved. It was only after he was gone that she realized there was something in her hand, that he had put something there. She opened her hand and looked. It was a five-baht piece. Bus fare was only two baht, and she had seven and a half, and he had given her a five-baht coin. When he said "*kao rot*," he didn't mean "take the bus," or "get on the bus." He meant "here's fare for the bus."

She stood there and looked at the coin in her open hand, and then down the road, where there was no longer any trace of the taxi. She was overwhelmed. She could hardly believe what had happened. The next thought she had was, wow, my instincts were right. I made the right decision. I had a hunch, and I followed it, and I was right.

She felt blessed. She had that grateful feeling again, the same one she had when she got back onto the raft. She thought, Ciara was there for me then, and this taxi driver was here for me now. What if there were always someone to help me when I needed it? What if everything I needed would always be within reach? What if that were really true?

She got on the bus, and she felt so good that it hardly bothered her when the bus conductor kept leaning over her seat and "accidentally" bumping into her.

Chapter 21

On her last day of school, at morning *kaotao*, Tamar was forced to make an impromptu speech. Ajahn Prichawat called her up during the announcements, and asked her to say a few words, over the PA system, to the whole school, with no preparation whatsoever.

She was startled, but she managed, in Thai, to say a few things, about its having been a great year, everyone's having been so kind and helpful, Thailand and Thai people being wonderful. She said things she knew she would be expected to say, but she realized as she said them that she meant them. It had been a great year, and they had been very good to her.

People said goodbye to her all day, often in English. Some gave her little presents, like pencils or Hello Kitty erasers. It made her very happy. She hadn't realized they cared that much. She felt she would miss her Thai life.

She had thought she would be happy to be rid of her school uniform, but when she went home and took it off, she decided to keep it. She was glad not to have to wear it anymore, but she couldn't seem to throw it away.

She savored every bite of dinner that night. Mehbahn made her favorite fresh coconut ice cream for dessert, and plenty of *ngaw* on the side. Everyone was there, even Papa and PiOhn.

They took pictures and made sure they had her address. She told them in Thai how grateful she was to them, and *wai*-ed everyone.

The whole family gathered in the front yard the next morning as PiTey drove Tamar to the FSA office for the last time. All of her sisters gave her little gifts as she got in the car. She was surprised to see how sad they all looked, even Mama and Papa. Everybody waved as PiTey backed the car out of the driveway into the *soi*. They turned onto *Tanon Chulalongkorn* for the last time, and Tamar fastened her eyes to everything she saw. She was ready to go back home now, to be in America again, but she wanted to remember everything.

There was a lot of traffic at the FSA office. People were being dropped off in cars and *dtukdtuks* and then herded onto buses and vans to go the airport. Everyone was saying goodbye and exchanging addresses. There was hugging and crying everywhere. Tamar made sure she found Fransje and Noelle and Duncan and got their addresses before she boarded the U.S. bus.

On the way to the airport, none of them spoke. They just looked out the windows and breathed in the Bangkok fumes.

On the plane, Tamar sat by the window again, with Ciara sitting next to her. Ben was just across the aisle. She looked at him, and he smiled at her.

"Do you still think Nebraska is boring?" she asked him.

"Yes, but it doesn't sound so bad now."

"So you won't mind telling me some Nebraska stories later?"

"Not if you'll tell me some L.A. and New York stories."

"Deal."

Tamar stared out the window as they taxied down the runway and then took off. She watched everything get smaller, first people, then cars, then buildings. Then they were out over the water, heading into the clouds.

She thought about PiJai, Pat and Nong, about Mehbahn and having servants, about Thai swordfighting and Ajahn Prichawat and creepy Ajahn Aroon. She thought about playing checkers and Dunkin' Donuts and the monsoon and the week she didn't need a handkerchief. She thought about *Songkran*, and Selena, and Ciara and Ben. She thought about Bangkok taxi drivers and bamboo rafts and she began to feel a kind of certainty, something indestructible inside her.

She thought about the Imperial Hotel, and her father and his new, fifth wife, and her mother and David and her half-siblings and her stepsiblings and all the rest. She thought about lands of the free and cities of angels and people and sadness and danger and fear and that feeling, that conquering hero feeling she'd had on the dock.

She thought about being seven years old, and seeing all the lights of Los Angeles for the first time. She remembered how small she felt, how alone in the vastness of it, and how lost and frightened it made her, and she realized something she didn't quite understand.

She still felt small, and fragile. She knew she could easily be smashed on the rocks like those bamboo rafts, but she had made a discovery, or rather, two. She had something inside her, an instinct that could guide her in the right direction, and there was something else, a sort of magic in the world that could bring help when she needed it. Somehow, these two things allowed her to think of boundlessness and unpredictability, even of sadness and pain, and to feel, not fear, but something like excitement. It was the feeling of being about to take an important test, or about to step on stage, or to start a race. It was anticipation, wanting to see what was going to happen, and wanting to find out how well she could do.

She didn't understand it. It didn't seem to make much sense, but it made her feel strong. She felt that no matter what happened, she could face it. She could feel things, even difficult things, and not run away. She could stand in the midst of emptiness and not be lost. It was that conquering hero feeling again, only deeper.

She watched everything go white as they climbed into the clouds, and another feeling, one of satisfaction, of accomplishment, came over her. She had come to Thailand wanting adventure, and she had found it, and now she was bringing it home.

Thank you for reading *Floating on Bamboo*! If you enjoyed it, or even if you didn't, please post a review on goodreads.com or amazon.com or kobo.com or Apple Books or wherever you read reviews, and share your opinion with the world.

Someone at this very moment is trying to decide whether or not to buy this book, and a review from you could help that person immensely.

Please visit esteigerandco.com if you would like to know more about author Erika Maren Steiger and her other books.

Acknowledgements

If I were to list all the people I should thank, the acknowledgements would require a separate book, so I will mention only a few: Aimee Liu, for allowing me to see a professional novelist at work, and for being so kind to me; Arlene Fink, for always being inspiring as well as fun, and for sending so much employment my way; my sister, Laura Yanovich, for always keeping my feet close to the ground, if not on it; my father, Paul E. Steiger, for sharing with me his love of and respect for language and his distaste for literary parlor tricks, and my mother, JoAnn McKenna, for incomparable support in innumerable ways, and for being the best possible role model a stubborn, unpredictable, driven, changeable, romantic, pragmatic and generally incomprehensible girl like me could have.

www.ingramcontent.com/pod-product-compliance
Lightning Source LLC
Chambersburg PA
CBHW032014170626
46807CB00006B/2799